MW01702177

WHERE THE LIGHT BEGINS

JESSICA GRAYSON

Purple Fall
Publishing

Published in the United States by Purple Fall Publishing. Purple Fall Publishing and the Purple Fall Publishing Logos are trademarks and/or registered trademarks of Purple Fall Publishing LLC.

Cover Design by Maria Spada

PRINTED IN THE UNITED STATES OF AMERICA

DEDICATION

To my husband: You are not just my husband, you are my best friend and my rock. Thank you for all your love and support. I love you more than words can ever say.

-Jessica Grayson

CHAPTER 1

ELENA

My heart hammers as my new master secures the slave collar around my neck. Two claw-tipped fingers under my chin lift my face to his. The Craven's lips pull back in a feral snarl, baring two rows of sharp fangs as his yellow cat-like eyes rake over my form with a lust-filled gaze.

I dart a glance around the room, searching for anything I might be able to use as a weapon. But this is a Pleasure House. The owners know better than to place anything in these areas that slaves might use to escape.

Fear tightens my chest as I study him and his partner. With pointed cat-like ears, their faces appear feline, and their noses are a bit broader than a Terran's. Their bodies are covered in a short layer of black and white fur in a striped pattern like a white tiger, long tails flicking agitatedly behind them as their golden cat eyes study me intently.

What concerns me most is the way they stare at me like predators assessing their prey.

I shift on the bedding and the clink of the chain around my ankle reminds me that even if I somehow managed to subdue my new masters, I would probably be unable to escape before anyone noticed.

The first one slips his clawed hand into my long, brown hair, lifting it to his face and inhaling deeply. A rumbling growl vibrates in his chest. "A fine purchase, do you not agree?"

His partner nods in approval. "Indeed." As his gaze settles on my face, he cocks his head to the side. "What is wrong with her eyes? Why are they brown instead of green?"

The first one shrugs. "Perhaps this V'loryn is defective."

Panic snakes through me and a bead of sweat trickles down my spine. They think I'm V'loryn. My masters before thought this, as well. They had no idea I was Terran.

No one does.

The V'loryns look remarkably like my people but taller and with glowing green eyes, pointed Elf ears, and three slight cranial ridges on their foreheads.

Since I have none of those features, I'm not quite sure how I'm mistaken for them, but I am.

"It matters not," the second one says. "She will still bring us many credits."

My entire body is shaking as his palm slides up my thigh and he grips my leg firmly. "I believe I will be the first to sample you, pet. To make sure our customers are not disappointed."

The one holding my chain leans toward me, drawing in a deep breath. "Your fear smells delicious."

A hot puff of air skitters across my skin as he scents me, and I'm acutely aware of just how little clothing I'm wearing. The top is a black leather bra, and the bottom is a matching skirt that only goes to mid-thigh with two long slits up each side to my hips.

His other hand grips my chin firmly, and he rubs his thumb roughly across my lower lip. "So soft and pliable, aren't you?" He chuckles darkly. "I believe you will be a favorite with our clients."

Ice cold fear floods my veins. Prior to this, I've always been placed in the pleasure simulator by my previous masters, but it looks like my new ones want to use and sell me in the flesh to customers. If this is my life, I don't want it. I'd rather die fighting.

His thumb mashes my lips again, and I open my mouth and then clamp my jaws shut, biting as hard as I can.

A pained howl erupts from his throat a moment before something hard connects with my jaw, sending me flying back.

Pain explodes across the back of my skull as I hit the wall. I struggle to remain conscious as my mind floats in the place between wakefulness and dreams. My head falls back as I lose the battle and fall away into unconsciousness.

Strong arms encircle me as I fall into my dream. I lean back into the arms of a man wrapped in shadow. Although I cannot see his face, I know he is not Terran. He is something... other.

I turn back to look up at him, only able to make out the pointed tip of one ear. "You came to me," I whisper. "I knew you would find me when I needed you."

He holds me tight against him and whispers in my ear, his voice smooth, deep, and achingly familiar. "I will always find you, my Si'an T'kara."

Si'an T'kara. Although I do not know what these words mean, I realize they need no translation to be understood. They call to something deep in my soul.

"Stay with me," I whisper. "Don't leave me here alone."

"You are mine," he says softly. "I will not leave you."

. . .

My eyes snap open as I come back into awareness. I lift my head, but everything feels off balance and wrong as I twist onto my side, feeling out with my other hand only to have another hard blow to my stomach. "You sl'evak!" my new master bellows as he grabs my forearm in a bruising grip and jerks me up to standing.

His other hand comes down hard at the back of my neck, and a sharp sting pierces the skin at my nape. I reach back only to feel something hard. I pull it away and gasp when I notice the dart; a drop of blood drips off the needle as it falls from my hand to the floor.

My heart hammers as I realize it's a breaking dart. The Masters use it to pacify slaves. It takes away their sight temporarily so they cannot fight back.

Despair wars with anger inside me. I'm chained here. It's not as if I could escape, anyway.

The masters chuckle darkly. "We will have fun with this one."

Darkness creeps in at the edges of my vision, and my head begins to swim as the breaking dart toxin takes effect.

Panic rips through me. I don't want to be unconscious and at the mercy of these monsters. I push myself up to standing and race away, only to feel the hard tug of the chain around my ankle. I lurch forward, falling to the ground, barely managing to catch myself before I face plant on the floor.

When I lift my head, my vision is completely gone. A wave of dizziness washes through me as I fight to stay conscious as the toxin works its way through my system.

My master rages behind me, and despite knowing how futile it is, I struggle against the unforgiving bite of metal around my ankle, trying to scramble away.

A rush of air fills the room and suddenly booted steps enter. They stop in front of me. "How dare you harm a female," a man's voice growls above me.

The scent of warm cinnamon touches my nostrils, and I reach my hand out, touching the hard toe of a boot. "Please," I whimper, praying this man is some sort of savior. "Help me."

"This is a place of business," my master yells. "You have no right to—"

"I am T'Hale Vanek of the Great House A'msir. I have *every* right to enforce the laws of V'lora on this station, you Craven scum." He growls low in his throat. The sound vicious and full of seething rage. "You will die for keeping slaves."

I was right. He is my savior.

Despite the haze of fog that surrounds my brain, I realize his voice sounds familiar, but I can't quite place it.

"Please, no!" one of the Craven masters cries out.

A low rumbling growl fills the air and the boot pulls away from my grasp. A rush of air moves past me and my master screams in fear a moment before I hear a harsh ripping sound followed by a splash of liquid slapping against the floor. A choked gurgling sound fills the room before falling silent.

The booted steps approach. A warm hand touches my chin as the smell of warm cinnamon floods my senses.

The pull of the breaking dart toxin is too hard to resist, and my eyes close as my head falls back as I fight to remain conscious. "Please, don't hurt me," I barely manage.

"I am Vanek and I would never harm you," he says, and my heart stutters and stops as the realization hits me.

I understand now why I recognize his voice. It belongs to the man I've seen in my dreams for so many years.

"You are safe," he murmurs. "I'm taking you back to my

ship. Do not worry. My people are allies with yours. I'm here to take you home."

"Home..." The word escapes my lips as the gentle lull of the breaking dart toxin begins to pull me under.

Unable to even open my eyes, I reach my hand out blindly, and he takes it in his own.

"What is your name?"

"Elena," I barely manage.

His hand is much larger than mine; his skin is soft and smooth beneath my palm. A wave of warmth and comfort flows through me from his touch. "Stay with me," I whisper, wondering if this is simply another dream. "Please, don't leave me here alone."

"I will not leave you," he whispers softly.

A tear escapes my lashes and rolls gently down my cheek. "I knew you would find me when I needed you," I whisper as I fall away into oblivion.

CHAPTER 2

VANEK

"Contact the Healer!" I snap at one of my men. "Tell her to meet us at the airlock! Now!"

A cacophony of sounds and voices surrounds me, and the familiar stench of poorly recycled air fills my lungs with each inhalation as I race out of the Pleasure House to the station's hangar.

I rush past the bright flashing lights and neon signs lining the promenade that promise customers all kinds of illegal indulgences. The crowd parts quickly as I charge through. No one wants to anger a V'loryn or get in our way. Especially not on a station like this.

One that is violating several of the laws that govern V'loryn space, any of which have a high probability of execution as punishment for breaking them.

My kind do not tolerate slavery; the punishment for trafficking slaves is immediate death without trial.

I glance down at the Terran female in my arms, praying that she is all right.

As soon as I reach my ship, I slam my hand on the airlock panel and it whooshes open to reveal Healer L'iral. Her eyes widen as she glances down at the Terran female in my arms.

"Follow me," she calls over her shoulder. "Quickly."

We rush down the hallway to the med bay. The crisp sparkling floors and panels are a welcome sight after being on the filthy and rusted station. L'iral gestures to the Med Repair Unit (MRU), and I gently place the female inside it.

"What happened to her?"

"I do not know. She went unconscious right after we rescued her."

L'iral studies the scanner as it runs over Elena's still form. "Did you find any other Terrans?"

I shake my head. "Not yet."

The reason we came to this station was because we'd heard rumors of Terran slaves here. As part of our alliance with their race, we agreed to help locate their missing people. They report that over the past fifty cycles, they've had several ships disappear en route between Terra and Mars.

A few Terrans have recently been discovered that had disappeared all that time ago but had been kept in stasis sleep for the past several decades. And because so much time had passed, a few of them returned to Terra only to find that their families and friends were either aged or already long gone.

As I stare down at her form, I wonder how long it has been that Elena has been missing.

"She has breaking dart toxin in her system," L'iral says. "She also has several fractures, some new and some already healing."

I clench my jaw as murderous rage moves through me. I turn to my personal guard, Garen. "Search the entire station for anymore slaves—Terran or otherwise. Any slavers are to be executed on sight."

"Of course, T'Hale." He dips his chin firmly and then leaves to do as I command.

L'iral looks at me. "The MRU is already working to heal her, but it will be a few hours."

My heart clenches as I study Elena's unconscious form. My gaze travels over her long, dark hair, her softly arched brows, and the round shells of her ears.

Like most Terran females, she is smaller than a V'loryn female. Our people weigh two to three times what hers do, and as I think on all her fractures, I cannot imagine how she endured the beatings from her masters.

I abhor slavery. Closing my eyes against the pain, I think of all the slaves we were unable to rescue in time during my cycles of service on the V'loryn Defense Force. I vow that we will not leave this station until every area is thoroughly searched and all the slaves held here are freed.

I turn to L'iral. "Contact the Terran embassy on V'lora. Let them know that we have located one of their people. Send her information to them so they can try to identify her and locate her family."

"Of course, T'Hale."

As I glance down at the female again, she begins to stir. "L'iral?"

The Healer moves to the MRU, frowning as she studies the readout. "The toxin seems to have worked its way out of her system faster than I anticipated. Her fractures appear to already be healed as well."

L'iral taps on the control panel. A sharp hiss of air escapes as the casing snaps open and lifts away.

Elena's eyelids flutter open. Warm, brown eyes blink up at me in fear. "Please," she says weakly. "Don't hurt me."

My heart stops, and I've suddenly forgotten how to speak.

Si'an'inamora. The ancient V'loryn words echo in my mind, and my world shifts in an instant.

She is my *Si'an T'kara*—my Fated One.

This altered state ripples through me, engulfing me completely and irrevocably. She is mine, and I am hers.

"I will not harm you," I speak softly. "My vow."

CHAPTER 3

ELENA

I open my eyes, and my heart stops when I see a man with glowing green eyes and pointed elf ears staring down at me in concern.

I'm lying in a bed. A screen overhead displays an outline of my body and several strange glyphs I can't read. From the crisp scent of antiseptic in the air and the meticulously polished walls and floors, this looks like some sort of medical center.

"How are you feeling?" the man asks, and I inhale sharply at the familiar sound of his voice.

"Vanek," I whisper his name as my memories return. "You came for me."

Tears fill my eyes as I reach out to him, needing to know that he's real, and not just a product of my imagination. I'm so afraid this is all a dream and that I'll wake at any moment back in a cage or a cell. "Is this real?"

I recognize his race as V'loryn. I've met a few of his kind that were held as slaves.

He's taller than any Terran man I've ever seen. Strong, broad shoulders taper to a narrow waist. He's dressed only in a dark tunic, pants, and boots. The material hides nothing of his lean, muscular form beneath.

His glowing, green eyes observe me as I continue to study him. He has short, dark-brown hair, warm tan skin, and a light scruff of dark brown beard that covers his square, masculine jaw. He has three slight cranial ridges on his forehead that start between heavy-set brows. One goes straight up to his hairline and the other two spread out like a *V* to his temples. He's so handsome, my cheeks heat under the intense scrutiny of his gaze.

"Yes," he replies softly. "You are safe now, Elena."

I've heard that V'loryns are incapable of emotions, but I don't think this is entirely true. Vanek's face is a perfect stoic mask, but it is easy to read the kindness and the emotion behind his eyes as he studies me in concern.

"You are Terran, are you not?"

"Yes." He's the first to recognize what I am. "Have you seen others like me?"

"Many. My people are allies with yours."

"How is that possible?" I stare at him in confusion. "My people have never had any contact with aliens before."

His brow furrows deeply. "You must have been taken before First Contact. Tell me: what is your full name and information? I must contact your embassy to let them know you've been found."

"My name is Elena Castillo. I'm in the Terran Space Program. I was assigned to the terraforming project on Mars. First Contact? What are you talking about?"

"The Mars Science Station sent a signal into deep space, alerting us to your presence and leading us to your home world. It was a few cycles ago, but we have formed an alliance since then."

"That can't be right," I murmur, more to myself than to him. "I haven't been awake longer than six months. I—" I stop abruptly as dread trickles down my spine. "What year is it?"

He frowns. "I... do not know the Terran Standard year. I only know the cycle according to V'lora—my home world."

A V'loryn woman with short, black hair steps out from behind him. "I am Healer L'iral. I realize this may seem a bit overwhelming, but I need you to answer a few questions so we can contact your people. "Do you remember anything about how you were taken?"

"I-I was in stasis sleep on the way back home from Mars. But when I woke up, I was in a cage on an alien ship. I don't know what happened to my crew." Tears sting my eyes, but I blink them back. "That was about six months ago, I think. I haven't seen any other Terrans since then. But I just assumed it hadn't been very long, but it could have been years..." My voice trails off as the weight of this knowledge hits me full force. I turn back to Vanek. "The other Terrans you've seen? Were they slaves, as well?"

"No. But there were rumors Terrans were being held on this station—sold into slavery. So, we came to investigate."

I open my mouth to speak, but another V'loryn with short, brown hair walks in. He's dressed in dark pants and a deep crimson tunic with something that looks like a Terran panther embroidered in golden thread across his chest. Despite his neutral expression, his glowing green eyes widen slightly when he notices me.

He bows low to Vanek. "T'Hale, we have cleared the rest of the establishment, and liberated fifty-two slaves."

"Did you find any more Terrans?"

"No."

"Have all the slavers been executed?" Vanek asks.

"Yes, T'Hale. And all their captives have been boarded on

the ship. I told them we would take them to V'lora and then help them to return to their homes."

Vanek dips his chin firmly. "Good. Then are we ready to disembark?"

"Yes, T'Hale. We should be leaving at any moment."

"Bring any who are injured here to the med bay."

"Of course, T'Hale."

When the man leaves, I turn back to Vanek. "T'Hale? Is that like a Lord?"

"From what I understand of this Terran term, it is… similar."

Healer L'iral interrupts. "I understand you probably have many questions, and we will be glad to answer them, but first, I believe you should eat and then rest." She turns to a display screen beside her and taps on the controls. "The MRU has healed your injuries, but your body still requires rest."

"My family," I start. "My older sister and my dad… can you contact them for me?"

She nods. "We have already sent some of your information to the Terran Embassy on V'lora—our home world. Now that we have your full name, we will send it as well so they can locate your family." She pauses. "In the meantime, we are on our way back to V'lora. We should arrive there in three days."

The sound of the engines spinning up thrums along the metal hull, echoing throughout the ship. An automated voice begins a countdown over the ship's speakers.

I notice a window across the way and stare out at the blackened void, punctuated by the light of a thousand stars, and watch as they begin to blur into streaks of yellow and white flying past the viewscreen.

I turn to Vanek. "How long does it take to travel from V'lora to Terra?"

"The journey is—"

A deafening boom explodes. The ship pitches to one side, sending me flying from the bed.

Vanek catches me in his arms, wrapping them securely around me as we fly toward the opposite wall. He twists at the last moment and his back slams against the bulkhead, shielding me from the brunt of the impact.

His eyes are wide as he quickly taps the communicator on his wrist and speaks into the display. "Garen, what happened?"

"Sabotage, T'Hale. They must have placed an explosive device on the hull while we were docked. We're running a sweep for any—"

Another explosion rocks along the hull and a flash of light fills the room a moment before everything goes dark.

CHAPTER 4

VANEK

When I awaken, it's to a dark, cramped cell. As my mind slowly comes back into awareness, my nostrils flare at the putrid scent of filth and blood that fill the air. I notice something tight around my neck, and when I reach up, I feel a metal slave collar.

Panic tightens my chest when I realize Elena is not here. Neither is my crew.

Movement in the corner of my eye draws my attention, and I notice a *Kragen* and two *Tauros* across the way. Each of them studying me warily.

"There was a female with me. Have you seen her?"

The closest Tauro shakes his head, and I notice one of his curled horns is broken and missing.

The Kragen moves a bit closer, his eight tentacles undulating as he moves across the floor. "A female you say?" he cocks his head to one side. "Where?"

A door whooshes open and light pierces the darkness as two Craven step inside. One of them carrying Elena.

I rush toward the front of the cell, calling out her name, but she does not answer.

Rage fills me, and I growl at the Craven as they approach. "Give her to me," I seethe. "Now."

"Stand back," the one carrying her snarls. "Or I'll place her in a different cell."

I move to the back of the cage, baring my fangs and extending my claws. My every muscle is tense, readying to strike, when the Craven presses a button on his belt, sending a shock of electricity straight through me.

My back arcs, and I fall to the floor as intense pain rips through my body.

When it finally stops, I watch as the Craven tosses Elena's unconscious form into the cell. Regaining my strength, I rush to her side, dropping to my knees beside her. "Elena." I struggle to hide the panic in my voice. "Elena, wake up."

"Get back, V'loryn," the Kragen growls behind me. "The female is mine."

One of his whip-like tentacles wraps around her ankle.

Anger burns through my veins like fire.

How dare he touch her!

Lightning fast, I extend my nails into lethal claws, and slice straight through his slimy flesh.

He shrieks and jerks away as his severed appendage slaps to the floor with a sickening squelch. He skitters to the opposite wall as I growl low in my throat.

I would finish the job and kill him without hesitation if I was not worried that the masters might punish me for killing their property by either hurting Elena or separating us.

Making sure to place myself protectively between her and them, I level an icy glare at the Kragen and the two Tauros. "If you dare try to touch her, I will end you," I snarl. "This female is mine, and she is under my protection. Do you understand?"

The Kragen, still oozing thick, green blood, nods quickly while the two Tauros stare at me in wide-eyed disbelief before nodding in agreement.

A deep growl rumbles in my chest as I bare my fangs, reminding them which of us is the superior predator here.

Elena shivers slightly, drawing my attention back to her.

Quickly, I remove my tunic, draping it over her smaller form. There is nowhere to sit in this cell but on the floor. I settle beside her and level another glower at my cellmates, growling in warning.

They lower their eyes and remain in their positions along the opposite wall.

Satisfied they will not challenge me, I turn my attention back to her. I brush her long, brown hair back from her face and study her closely. My gaze travels over the curved shells of her ears, her golden skin, softly arched brows, and her full, pink lips.

Fierce protectiveness fills me as I gather her in my arms, holding her close to my chest. I sit with my back to the wall so I can keep a watchful eye on our cellmates.

She is smaller than a V'loryn female, but all Terrans are. As I hold her slight weight in my arms, I am reminded again of how fragile they are compared to my kind.

My people possess two to three times the strength of hers, and our body mass is much more dense, due to the higher gravity on our home world. I trail my hand lightly down her arm, noting the heavy bruising on her skin in the shape of a large handprint.

A rage-filled growl rises in my chest at the thought of all she must have endured at the hands of the Craven masters. I trace my fingers over the delicate bones of her wrists and hands. I know from firsthand experience with her kind that Terrans are much stronger than they appear, but still… the visible bruising all along her skin makes me worry.

What other injuries has she sustained that I cannot see?

She is of similar height and build as Elizabeth—the Terran bondmate of my best friend Marek.

He is the only other V'loryn, besides me, that has found his Si'an T'kara outside of our race.

Marek told me the pull of the fate bond was strong when he first met Elizabeth, but I never expected it to feel like this.

My people are taught to suppress our emotions, binding them deep within ourselves at all times. And yet, as I look at Elena, I can feel my tightly held controls beginning to slip.

Unbridled rage fills me as I stare the Kragen and two Tauros. Something dark and primal unfurls deep within me, clawing its way to the surface, and demanding to be freed. If they so much as look at her wrong, I will end them.

They stay along the opposite wall, knowing better than to challenge me. In the metal panels behind them, I see my terrifying reflection.

Instead of their normal, glowing green, my eyes are obsidian black, and my fangs are bared in feral snarl as a deep growl of warning vibrates in my chest.

Elena stirs in my arms, and I turn my attention back to her.

Because my people are natural touch telepaths, I hold her carefully, making sure to keep my mental shields firmly in place to prevent the accidental sharing of thought or emotion through the *al'nara*—the mind link. We are taught from an early age to create the mental barrier to shield ourselves from accidental telepathic exchange through touch.

It is normally forbidden among my people to touch someone who is neither bondmate nor family, but as I glare at the others, I want to leave no doubt in their minds that she is mine and I have claimed her.

Her eyelids flutter open. Warm, brown eyes blink up at me. "Vanek," she says weakly. "What happened?"

"Slavers sabotaged my ship and somehow rendered us unconscious. We are in a cell on their vessel."

She inhales sharply. "We've been captured?"

Reluctantly, I nod.

All the color drains from her face as she curls her body into mine, instinctively seeking safety and protection. "What are we going to do?"

The cargo bay doors whoosh open again, and two more Craven masters walk in. Their golden eyes snap to mine as they approach the cage.

I stand, and pull Elena behind me to shield her.

The first one turns to the other. "You're right. They are a mated pair. Look how protective he is of her. They will bring us thousands of credits if we enter them in the Great Hunt."

Panic steals my breath. I've only ever heard rumors of the Great Hunt from other slaves we have rescued. And if the stories I have been told are true, we are in even greater danger than I first realized.

The closest Craven flares his nostrils, scenting the air. His eyes roll up in the back of his head before he turns a lustful gaze to her. "V'loryn females always smell sweeter than the others, but this one even more so."

He thinks she's V'loryn. I do not correct him. If he knew she was Terran, she would be in even more danger than she is now. The A'kai hunt her kind, and pay thousands of credits for them. They want them for their blood. My gaze travels over the slave master. As bad as the Cravens are, the A'kai are far worse.

I will tear out his throat if he dares try to touch her.

"I am Vanek, T'Hale of the Great House A'msir," I state firmly. "If you free me and the female, I will make sure you are paid handsomely for your troubles."

He narrows his eyes. "More likely I will end up dead," he counters. "The moment I came to collect my reward you would have me executed for being a slaver."

I give him an impassive look, betraying nothing, but he is right.

I would execute him at the first opportunity.

The punishment among my people for keeping slaves is death.

A sinister grin curls his lips. "I have no need of a reward for your return to V'lora. You and the female will earn us thousands of credits in the Great Hunt."

"You cannot do this," I growl.

"Oh, I can and I will, *T'Hale of Great House A'msir*," he says my title mockingly. "And you will do exactly as you're supposed to, and not give us any trouble. If you do, we will take your female from you."

"If you want someone to participate in the Great Hunt, take me, not her," I demand. "Let her go."

"Why do you think we returned your female to you in the first place? V'loryn males are notoriously difficult to control. The only thing that makes a V'loryn male comply is the threat of harm to one of his kin... especially a female."

Elena remains silent. The acrid scent of her fear permeates the entire cell, heightening my protective and possessive instincts.

My hands curl into fists at my side. "If anything happens to her—"

"You see?" He grins. "That's why we threw her in with you." He gestures to the Kragen and Tauros. "Having them here was a test, to make sure you felt protective of her... kept her safe from them."

My fangs extend into sharpened points as I contemplate exactly how I will kill them all once I'm free.

As if sensing my intent, he snarls. "You make one wrong

move and I will leave your precious female alone with the others."

Rage boils deep within.

He narrows his eyes. "If you win, maybe you will get to keep her. Depends on what the crowd wants though."

My heart pounds at the anger flooding my system. I want nothing more than to rip this male to shreds and tear his beating heart out with my bare hands.

Without warning, he presses the control button for Elena's collar, and she cries out in pain a moment before slumping to the floor behind me, falling unconscious.

An angry roar rips from my throat a moment before he presses another button and my collar begins to tingle with electricity.

"Relax or I will immobilize you as well, leaving her vulnerable to your cellmates," the Craven says darkly. "You need to remember who is in charge here, V'loryn."

He crosses his furry black and white striped arms over his chest. "You thought you were so smart," he sneers. "Well, look where you are now." He leans in, and flashes a toothy grin. "I thought you should know that our Healer scanned you. We know about your addiction."

Ice fills my veins. Neural relaxers are as dangerous as they are illegal, but I can hardly sleep without them. They are highly addictive, and now he knows my weakness. I cannot go long without them before suffering withdrawals.

He pulls two pills from his pocket and throws them at me. They bounce off my chest onto the floor.

"Hmph," he grumbles to himself. "Never thought a V'loryn would become addicted to this stuff." He smirks. "Don't worry. I will give you enough to get you through. Can't have you going through withdrawals during the games, now, can we?"

He starts to leave, but I call out. "Take the others. Put them in a different cell."

He pauses a moment, considering.

"You know what I will do to protect her," I threaten. "If you leave them in here with us, I will end them all before we even reach the arena."

He gestures to the other slaver behind him, and together, they usher the Kragen and two Tauros out of the cell.

After they are gone, I pull Elena into my arms, holding her close to my chest and praying she awakens soon.

Her eyelids flutter open and closed as she goes in and out of consciousness, fighting the aftereffects of the shock collar.

A long tail snakes through the cell bars and curls around my pills. I watch in anger as an Anguis in the right cell begins to pull them back through to his cage.

I whip my arm out to catch his tail. His scales are rough against my palm as I squeeze tight.

He screeches in alarm as I crush his bones beneath my grip, forcing him to relinquish the neural relaxers.

I quickly pocket them with my other hand, saving them for later.

He rips his tail from my grasp, gasping in horror as the end remains completely limp. He bares his fangs in a low hiss, and his eyes dart to my mate. "You will pay for this, V'loryn."

I bare my fangs in return. "If you dare try to touch her, it will be *your* end, Anguis."

He lowers his gaze and moves to the opposite side of his cell, as far from me as he can.

Reaching down, I gently brush the hair back from Elena's face. A tear escapes her lashes as she manages to open her eyes and look up at me. "Please," she barely manages. "Don't let them take me."

"I will die before I allow them to take you away from me, Elena. My vow."

Her small brow furrows softly as she studies me. "Something is wrong with me. I can hardly keep my eyes open."

"It is an effect of the shock collar," I explain. "Rest now. I will watch over you."

She nods weakly and then closes her eyes.

She shivers again and I pull her into my lap and wrap my arms around her to keep her warm. I am pleased when she stops shivering and relaxes against me.

The Lycaon in the cage beside us raises his head. His nostrils flare as he scents the air and his knowing eyes shift to me. "She is not V'loryn, is she?"

I answer with a low growl.

"Do not worry, V'loryn," he huffs. "Your secret is safe with me. I know what she is to you."

My heart stops.

He cannot possibly know this.

"I recognized the look in your eyes when they returned her to you. My kind have Fated mates, as well." He sighs heavily. "And my people do not hurt females, despite what you V'loryns think you know of us. Females are treasured in our culture, regardless of species."

All I have ever heard of Lycaons is that they are a warrior race. Similar to the Mosaurans but more savage. They prefer to hunt in their four-legged beast form and live in packs.

He continues. "The arena is no place for a Terran. They are a fragile species."

My eyes snap to him. "How do *you* know what she is? Have you seen others?"

"I saw one other like her." His expression sobers. "And I know the A'kai are searching for them and their world."

"Where did you see another Terran?" I ask.

"Vylax station. Two Mosaurans stole her from her A'kai master."

Relief fills me. "If the Mosaurans took her, then she is well. They abhor slavery as much as my people do."

"I only hope they got away safely." He darts a glance at Elena, lying unconscious in my arms. "You need to wean yourself off the neural relaxers before the games. Your addiction will get you killed."

"I know."

"Why do you take them?" he asks. "What is it that haunts you so much you cannot sleep?"

I close my eyes as the dark memories return. Drawing in a deep breath, I push them down. I cannot afford to think of this now. I meet his glowing, orange eyes evenly. "I do not know of what you speak."

"Whatever you say, V'loryn." He huffs and sits back against the bars of his cell. "Just make sure before we reach the arena you have tapered off enough to get by." His gaze flicks to Elena. "You will need to be at full strength if you are going to protect her."

He is right. I just pray there is enough time for me to free myself of this addiction completely before we are thrown into the arena.

"I can help you watch over her."

"No!" I snap as my possessive instincts flare.

"Fine," he growls. "But know this: when we are out there in the arena, you will need me V'loryn. If you want to keep her safe, I suggest you learn to accept help when it is offered."

"Since when do Lycaons offer help to Outsiders?" I counter. "Your kind are only loyal to your own packs."

"I already told you," he grinds out. "We are not the savages you believe us to be."

I narrow my eyes. "That remains to be seen."

Elena shifts slightly in my arms. I reach down and brush the hair back from her face, and her eyelids flutter open.

She blinks several times and looks up at me, her expression full of alarm.

"It is all right," I speak soothingly. "You are safe. The others have been removed from this cell."

CHAPTER 5

ELENA

I glance down at my body and realize I'm draped in an oversized shirt. "Did you… give me your clothes?"

He dips his chin in a polite nod. "You were cold; I was not. It seemed like a logical thing to do."

I offer him a faint smile. "Thank you, Vanek."

Although we have only just met, I feel as if I've known him forever. The sound of his voice is as familiar to me as my own. He makes me feel safe.

He opens his mouth to speak, but the cargo bay doors whoosh open, and two Craven step inside. One of them approaches our cell, his feline eyes locked on to mine. This one I've never seen before. He opens the cell door and points to me. "You. Come here."

Fear fills me when I detect the lust dancing behind his yellow eyes. Tears swim at the edge of my vision, but I blink them back. Despite my attempt to push down my panic, my entire body begins trembling.

I've been used several times in the pleasure simulators

before, but judging from the way this Craven is looking at me now, I doubt he'll use the sim to take me.

Lightning fast, Vanek grips my forearm and pulls me behind him, placing himself directly between me and the Craven. "You *will not* touch her."

"Step aside or I will blast you," he grinds out.

Without warning, Vanek rushes him. The Craven lunges back, slamming the cell door shut only a moment before Vanek reaches him.

Vanek's chest rises and falls as he levels an ice-cold glare at the two. "She is mine," he snarls. "I will not let you take her from me."

The cargo bay doors open and another Craven steps inside. He scowls at the others. "I already told you," he snaps. "The V'loryn female is off limits."

A sly smirk twists the first one's mouth as he exchanges a glance with his companion. "For now."

"Let us go"—Vanek growls—"or I promise you that once I am free, I will find you, and I will end you."

The closest one chuckles. "If you knew the kind of payout I am getting for two V'loryns, you would know it is well worth the risk to me."

Without another word, they turn to leave.

Vanek turns to me, his expression full of concern. "Are you all right?"

I nod, even though it's a lie. I'm terrified, but I learned long ago that tears and crying don't help.

"You should not keep threatening them. The Craven are extremely volatile and territorial," a deep voice sounds from the cell beside us. I turn in the direction of the sound and put my hand to my mouth to stifle a gasp at the heavily muscled man with glowing orange eyes, golden skin, slightly pointed ears, lethal claws, and sharp fangs. I don't know how I didn't notice this guy before. He's absolutely terrifying.

"I am aware," Vanek replies darkly as he moves to place himself directly between me and the man in the cell next to ours.

He's protecting me.

I don't know why, but I'm not going to question it. He's been nothing but kind and protective since we met. This is the first time I've had someone strong on my side, and even though I only just met him, I know that he will not harm me.

After all, for all intents and purposes, he's already proven more than once that he wants to protect me. And it can't be a coincidence that I dreamed of him before we met. My grandmother used to say that all dreams have meaning. And I believe that mine were so I would know that Vanek is a good person, and I can trust him.

I peer around Vanek at the other guy. I've never seen his species before. "What are you?"

"Lycaon," Vanek replies before the man can. "Savage, brutal beasts who thirst for blood and battle."

"You know nothing about me or my kin," the other man snarls.

"I know enough," Vanek grits through his teeth.

"And I've always heard your kind were completely devoid of emotion, but judging by your reaction to our captors, I realize now that is not true," the Lycaon counters.

Vanek narrows his eyes.

The Lycaon huffs out a frustrated breath. "We could be allies if you—"

A harsh snap fills the room and the cell walls, even the bars go completely dark, like some sort of barrier has been suddenly erected between them. I turn to Vanek. "What was that?"

"The masters have put up the barrier shields to prevent us from arguing or fighting with the others. They want us to be rested before the Great Hunt."

"What is the Great Hunt?"

"The ultimate illegal thrill," he says grimly. "Species from all over gather together to compete. Slaves are dropped into an arena to be hunted by others. The Hunters pay hundreds of thousands of credits to participate. They believe it is the ultimate challenge to hunt sentient prey."

I inhale sharply. "They're going to hunt us?"

He nods. "And if they catch us, they will kill us."

An involuntary shudder moves through me. "I don't want to die," I whisper more to myself than to him.

Of everything I've endured since I woke up as a slave, I can't imagine it all ending like this. Not now. Not after everything I've survived.

Tears sting my eyes, but I blink them back. I have to be strong.

"I will do all I can to keep you safe, Elena," Vanek says softly.

I can still hardly believe Vanek is even real. Part of me knows it's crazy to trust someone so quickly, but another part recognizes that I am about to be thrown into something far more dangerous than anything I've faced so far.

If I am going to survive, I have to trust someone, and I figure it might as well be him. I dreamed about him for a reason. Now, I want to know what it is. "Why are you helping me?"

CHAPTER 6

VANEK

I could tell her the truth, but I worry it would only add to her stress. If she knew she was my Si'an T'kara—my Fated One—she may fear I might try to force myself upon her. That is something I would never do, but she does not know this.

Besides, I could never take her as my mate. When my people take a bondmate, we form a permanent mental connection between us. It allows us to share emotions and thought. I have vowed never to take a bondmate. I would never want to subject someone to the nightmares that plague me. No one should ever have to experience what I went through.

I meet her gaze evenly as I prepare my half-truth. "I was sent by my emperor to find and rescue Terrans from the slave trade. Our people are allies. As such, it is only natural that I would help you."

Her warm brown eyes search mine, and I realize how easy it would be to become lost in their depths. If this is how

Marek felt around Elizabeth, before they were bonded, I do not know how he remained in her presence for so long without going mad.

Everything inside me want to claim her as mine. My eyes drift to the pulse artery along her neck. I long more than anything to sink my teeth deep in her flesh and seal her to me in the sacred blood ritual of the *S'acris*.

"What happens when we get to the arena for the Great Hunt?"

"I do not know. I have never seen a Great Hunt before. I have only heard of them."

What I do not tell her is that only one contestant can survive. The one who does is given their freedom. It is the ultimate prize for any slave. Many gladiators are placed in the Great Hunt by their masters. Even though the prize would be their freedom, the payout their masters would earn from forcing them to compete can be more than anything they would normally earn by having them fight in the gladiator pits. That is why many slavers risk their best fighters in the games.

As a result, our competition will not be easy. Many times, those being hunted will kill others to eliminate their competitors, increasing their chances of winning their freedom. I wish I did not have to share this with her, but she must understand what we will face.

"In the Great Hunt, not only must we worry about the Hunters but about the other players, as well."

"What do you mean?"

"It is not unusual for those being hunted to kill each other off to increase their own chances of winning the games."

"Why would they do that?"

"To win you must survive until the end." I give her a half-truth, not sharing that only one contestant will reach this point. "Once you do, you gain your freedom."

She looks down at the floor, her small brow furrowing deeply in contemplation. "You think we can make it?"

"My people are stronger and faster than most of the other races. We have an advantage over the others."

"You mean *you* have an advantage," she counters.

"No," I state firmly. "*We* do—you and me. We will make it to the end, and you will gain your freedom, and return to your people, Elena."

"Thank you, Vanek," she whispers softly. A tear slips down her cheek, but she quickly brushes it away.

Cautiously, I reach forward and tuck a stray tendril of hair behind her ear as I study her. I cannot even begin to imagine all she must have been through. If I could, I would kill every single person who has ever hurt her. I would protect her forever if I could. An uncomfortable knot forms in my chest when I remember that she can never truly be mine. I am too damaged and broken to take a bondmate. I would never subject anyone to my nightmares.

"You should rest, Elena. Sleep while you can. We both should."

She hugs her knees tight to her chest, curling in on herself as she lies on the floor with her back against the wall. I watch her close her eyes and listen to her breathing becoming soft and even as she drifts away.

Making sure to position myself between her and the cell door before lying down, I glance back at Elena and send out a silent prayer to the Goddess to grant me the strength to protect my Si'an T'kara. Even if she will never truly be mine, I will die before I allow anyone to harm her.

Drawing in a deep breath, I try to will myself to relax. Sleep is nearly impossible for me without the neural relaxers. I have become accustomed to using them nearly every night. It is the only way I can sleep without risking the nightmares that always seem to find me: the dark memories I cannot forget, no matter how hard I try.

I reach into my pocket and feel the two pills the Craven gave to me. I've already begun weaning myself off the relaxers over the past few months, but I worry I could still go through withdrawals. I curse myself for getting off of them sooner.

The temptation to take both pills would normally consume me, but not now. As I glance at Elena, I know I cannot fail her. I must remain awake and alert. I do not know when we are going to be dropped into the arena, and I cannot risk being under the influence of this drug when we are. She needs me, and I intend to make sure that, out of all the contestants, she will be the one left alive at the end of the Hunt.

Closing my eyes, I draw in a deep breath and allow myself to begin to drift away, praying the nightmares do not come.

Sleep claims me, and I fall into my nightmare. The one I know so well.

I open the cargo bay door, expecting to find cages full of slaves that I may rescue. Instead, an Aerilon female with violet skin, and silver-white hair lies on the floor, her broken wings splayed out beneath her.

I kill her Anguis captor, and drop to my knees beside her still form. Despair floods my veins when I notice the fang marks on her thigh from the Anguis. I am too late. Her fate has already been sealed.

Golden eyes full of tears stare up at me, and I gather her in my arms, helpless to do anything but watch as she dies a slow and painful death.

. . .

A sharp cry rings out, startling me back into full awareness. I spin toward Elena and find her thrashing on the floor.

I rush to her side, falling to my knees before her. Her eyes are closed, and I realize she is still asleep. Gently, I place a hand on her shoulder. "Elena, wake up," I speak softly. "You are having a nightmare."

CHAPTER 7

ELENA

A subtle hiss pierces the pitch-black darkness and ice-cold fear trickles down my spine. Something wet slicks up my neck, and I jerk back. "Your fear is delicioussss," a man's voice whispers behind me.

A strong hand grips my forearm in an iron vise, pulling me into a solid wall of muscle. Coarse scales scrape my skin like sandpaper.

"Let me go!" I cry out.

Panic fills me as my vision adjusts to the darkness, and I realize I'm back in the pleasure sim. An Anguis client stares down at me. With a cobra-like hood around his head, his vertically slit pupils are wide with lust as his forked tongue skates across my skin.

"I paid for my time in the pleasure simulator, slave. You are mine to do with as I please," he hisses.

"No!"

"Elena!"

My eyes snap open to find glowing, green ones staring down at me in concern.

Tears blur my vision as I dart a panicked glance around the cell, searching for any sign of the Anguis.

"You were having a nightmare," Vanek says.

Despite his words of reassurance, the fear is still rooted deep within, filling my veins with ice. I open my mouth to speak, but the words won't come.

Drawing in a shaking breath, I struggle to calm my heart rate and breathing as I push down my fear. Despite my attempts to hold in my tears, the first one escapes my lashes and rolls down my cheek.

Vanek cups my face. His gaze holds mine as he gently brushes the pad of his thumb across my skin, wiping away my tears. "I will keep you safe in the arena. My vow."

I lean into his touch. It's been so long since I could rely on anyone besides myself that I'd forgotten what it was to have someone be there for me.

A shiver runs through me, both from the cold and from the memory of my nightmare. Carefully, Vanek wraps an arm around my shoulders and pulls me close, enveloping me in warmth.

"I dreamed I was back in the pleasure simulators," I whisper. "It was… terrifying."

"I wish I could kill everyone who ever hurt you," he murmurs above me. "Know that I will do whatever it takes to keep you safe, Elena."

I lean against him and close my eyes. In my dreams, this is exactly what he would do. I was in love with the man in my dreams.

And maybe it's my dreams that make me feel the way I do, but I cannot deny that I'm drawn to him.

"Thank you," I reply softly.

Drawing in a deep breath, I force myself to focus. If we're

going to survive, I need to know as much about what we're going into as possible. I pull back just enough to look up at him. "Tell me everything you know about this Great Hunt."

He sighs. "I only know it is a test of strength, survival, and endurance."

"Do you know what kind of environment we'll be in?"

"The arena changes each cycle, from what I have been told." He looks at me. "Do you have any combat or survival training?"

"I was in the Terran Space Program. It was a requirement to learn those things."

"This is good."

"What about you?"

"All V'loryns serve in the V'loryn Defense Force for a five-cycle term. I finished my term only a few cycles ago."

"You were in the military?"

His gaze drifts to the opposite wall with a faraway look. "Yes."

I know that expression: the hundred-yard stare. The one people have after they've been through unimaginable trauma. I know better than to ask what it is that haunts him. If he wants to share, he will. If not… I'll respect his decision to keep it to himself.

After a moment, he turns to me. "What did you do in the Terran Space Program?"

"I was a botanist."

A hint of a smile quirks his lips. "My mother was a botanist, too."

"Oh?"

He dips his chin. "My earliest memories are of helping her tend to her *oralia* flowers. They are similar to Terran roses, but much larger."

"Roses are my favorite," I offer. "I grew an entire garden of them in the main atrium on Mars Colony." A wistful smile crests my lips as memories of vibrant blooms that had no right to exist in a place so barren fills my thoughts. "Technically, I wasn't supposed to do that."

He arches a curious brow. "Why?"

"Mars is a desert planet. It's wasteful to grow something that requires so much water to maintain, but I—" my voice hitches as I think of my mom. "I did it in memory of my mother." I swallow against the lump in my throat. "I grew them from the clippings I took from her own rose garden after she died."

Silence settles in the space between us as I choke back the tears threatening to erupt from deep within.

"My soul grieves with yours," Vanek says solemnly.

"Thank you," I barely manage to reply.

After a few moments, I'm able to speak again. "Do you still have your parents?"

He lowers his gaze. "My father is alive, but my mother died when I was young."

"My soul grieves with yours," I repeat his words to him.

Despite his impassive expression, sadness reflects behind his eyes. "Thank you." He pauses. "You should try to rest, Elena. I do not know exactly what awaits us, but I know we will need to be at full strength when we arrive."

As I lean against him, he wraps his arm around me, holding me close. I barely know this man, and yet, I trust him. Completely. Closing my eyes, I draw in a deep breath. The scent of warm cinnamon fills my senses and I realize it must be him.

The warmth of his body radiates to mine and, for the first time in a long time, I allow myself to drift away knowing that whatever happens, someone will be watching over me.

CHAPTER 8

VANEK

I glance down at Elena. Her eyes are already closed as she snuggles against me. I shift slightly and she nestles into my side, instinctively seeking warmth.

She is my Si'an T'kara. Already, I feel protective and possessive of her. I inhale deeply, drawing her delicate scent into my lungs. Because she is wearing my tunic, she already smells strongly of me. Something dark and primal unfurls from deep within as I glance at the pulsing artery along her neck.

The desire to sink my fangs deep into her flesh and claim her as my mate is nearly overwhelming.

I force myself to avert my eyes. I cannot give in to these primal instincts. She can never be mine. I am too broken to take a bondmate.

Gently, I brush the hair back from her face, tucking it behind her ear. She has been through much and deserves someone who is not damaged like me.

As I study the delicate curved shells of her ears and her

gently arched brows, I send a silent prayer to the Goddess, asking her to help me keep my Si'an T'kara safe.

All that matters is that she lives.

Hours pass before the barrier lifts from our cell, allowing us access to the others. The Lycaon flashes a wicked snarl in my direction when he sees me holding Elena as she sleeps. The Anguis, from the opposite cell, eyes her lasciviously. I bare my fangs in challenge, warning him to avert his gaze.

The cargo bay doors slide open and several Craven step inside. They line up in front of the cells, shock sticks at their sides. "Get up!" the nearest one calls out. "It is time to go!"

Elena's eyes snap open, her expression filled with fear as her eyes dart around the room. "What's going on?"

"I believe we have arrived," I explain. "Stay close to me and remember: tell no one you are Terran. They believe you are V'loryn. You must maintain this lie."

She nods.

One of the Craven opens the cell door and ushers us out into the hallway. I position myself as close to Elena as possible as we make our way to the airlock. A sharp hiss of air escapes as it opens, revealing a hangar bay of some sort.

Several ships of varying shapes and sizes are parked next to each other. All of them appear to be in excellent shape, suggesting their owners have wealth. I suppose this makes sense. The Great Hunt is known to attract only the wealthiest spectators and patrons.

My stomach roils at the thought of how many credits they must pay to witness such a brutal event.

My nostrils flare as I scent the air, surprised by how fresh it smells. Surely, we cannot be on a station. I suspect we are planetside somewhere.

A *Patiko* male rushes forward. His red tail feathers spread wide to show off his thick plumage and his beak-like face studies us appraisingly. He clasps his hands together in front of his chest and makes an excited chirping noise. "A mated pair?"

The closest Craven nods.

I do not correct him; neither does Elena. I want them to believe we are mated. They will keep us together because of this. They know V'loryns do not do well if separated from their bondmates.

The Patiko moves closer, his gaze traveling up and down Elena's form. He shakes his head emphatically. "This will not do. This will not do at all. They will need much better clothing."

He steps back, scratching at his chin as he assesses us. "Hmmm. I am Chylan." He spins on his heels. "Follow me."

One of the Craven follows behind us, his hand on the control of our collars to shock and immobilize us if we dare try anything. I force my expression to remain stoic, all the while mentally calculating the odds of success were I to attack the Craven anyway.

Elena moves closer to me as we walk. Fierce protectiveness fills me. It takes every bit of my control to not wrap a possessive arm around her waist and tug her to my side.

I hate the way several of the males we pass track her movements with lust-filled eyes.

CHAPTER 9

ELENA

The strange peacock-like alien rakes his eyes over us. His red tail feathers are spread wide. I've seen his kind before. They are called Patikos. I would probably think his crimson and gold coloring beautiful if I weren't so afraid.

He spins on his heels, and his tail feathers fold together with an audible snap as he calls over his shoulder, "Follow me."

I glance around the hangar, surprised by how full it seems. Several of the ships are unloading slaves, just like our vessel.

As we walk through the hangar, I try my best not to gawk at all the people. Many species I've never seen before are here. Tails, wings, claws, fangs, scales… I had no idea there was this much diverse life in the universe.

I observe several men staring at me with unmistakable lust in their gazes, and move closer to Vanek's side.

Chylan opens a door, and I gasp as bright light floods my vision.

When we step out of the hangar, it takes my eyes a moment to adjust to the brightness. I haven't been outside in so long. "Where are we?"

"I do not know," Vanek replies beside me.

The Craven and Chylan don't bother answering my question as they lead us.

Up ahead, I see several buildings constructed of dark gray metal. They are no more than two or three stories tall but tightly packed together. Although it's daylight, several neon signs blink above them.

We step onto a crowded street, following after several other slavers and their captors. Vendors with various carts full of wares line the pathways, calling out to try to attract customers.

The scent of smoked meats and spices hangs heavy in the air. The cobblestone paths are poorly kept and full of trash and litter.

We pass a pleasure house and a shiver of fear runs down my spine when Chylan stops in front of it. Panic hits me full force as dark memories fill my mind.

Chylan turns back to the Craven. "Did you want to leave her here to earn you a few credits before we begin? Some of the others have left their females here for the pleasure sims. Clients would pay lots of credits for her."

Ice fills my veins.

Vanek wraps a possessive arm around my waist and tugs me to him. A deep and menacing growl vibrates his chest. His eyes swirl from glowing green to obsidian black as he bares his fangs at the Patiko and the Craven. "If you dare try to touch her, I will end you."

Chylan steps back, his eyes blinking rapidly as he darts a helpless glance at the Craven.

The Craven steps forward. "Unfortunately, I cannot rent her out. He'll go mad if I do, and that would cost me even more credits." He shakes his head. "You know how possessive V'loryns are of their mates."

"Fine," the Patiko says. "Let us continue then."

Vanek's arm remains locked around me as we follow after him. "Do not worry," he whispers so low I nearly miss it. "If they dared try anything, I would be able to kill them both before I was immobilized."

I lift my gaze to him and find him with his normally impassive expression, but when his eyes meet mine, it is easy to see the murderous anger burning behind them. It doesn't scare me because I know his rage is directed at our captors, not me.

The Patiko leads us into a large building. Several slaves of various species with collars around their necks fill the space, most of them heavily muscled, reminding me of the gladiators I saw many times at the fighting pits.

We snake our way through the crowd and into a small room near the back. When we enter, I see only a small bed in a corner with a surprisingly plush-looking gray comforter and pillows. A tiny window to the outside has bars across it. A table and two chairs sit in the opposite corner.

Chylan gestures to a door across the way. "The cleansing room is in there." He turns to us. "This will be your room for the evening. I will come for you in the morning to get you ready for the crowd before the Hunt. Before I leave though, I must get your measurements."

He raises a small device and waves it over us both. It beeps once, and he dips his chin in an affirmatory nod. "Great. I believe I have all I need to get your clothing ready." He cocks his head to the side. "Food will be brought for you both shortly."

As he moves to the door, the Craven turns to us and

points a stern finger at Vanek. "Try to escape and I'll make sure you regret it."

Vanek responds by tightening his arm around my waist and narrowing his eyes.

Once the Craven and Chylan step out into the hallway, they seal the door shut behind them. A subtle click tells me we've been locked in, but I didn't expect anything less.

As soon as they're gone, I'm reluctant to pull away from Vanek, but there is no reason for me to be so close to him now that we're alone.

Before I can move away from him, he turns to me. "They believe we are a mated pair. We must encourage this belief, because they will keep us together for the Great Hunt."

"What do you mean 'keep us together?' "

"Tomorrow, they will drop all the contestants at various locations. This is done to spread everyone out and make it more challenging for the Hunters to... pick us off."

I swallow hard at the mere thought of being hunted as if I were an animal instead of a sentient being.

"Because they believe we are mated, they will keep us together." He sighs. "But this also makes us a bigger target. Hunters will be more tempted to go after us because it would mean two kills in one if we were discovered."

I inhale sharply. "How do you know this?"

"I have heard stories. The way the Craven spoke of us being a bonded pair confirmed what I have heard."

My mind begins to race even as my pulse pounds in my ears.

I still can't believe this is happening... that we're actually going to be hunted for sport.

Closing my eyes, I draw in a deep breath, attempting to push down my growing anxiety.

Being worried about something I have no control over will do me no good. I need to focus on the present. I need to keep my mind sharp to make sure I can survive whatever they throw at us in this Great Hunt.

My eyes dart to the bed, and I swallow hard. “How do we convince them we are a mated pair?”

Vanek’s expression is solemn as he takes my hand. “It is forbidden in my culture to touch one to whom you are neither bonded nor family.”

“Why?”

“My people are touch telepaths. Able to exchange thought and emotion through a simple act of touch.”

I frown as I glance at our hands. “I don’t… feel or sense anything like this.”

“Because we are also taught how to erect and maintain a mental transference shield to ensure that if we accidentally touch someone, we do not read their thoughts or emotions, and they cannot read ours either.”

“That sounds… exhausting.”

He arches a brow. “It is not as difficult as you might believe.” He entwines our fingers. “So… in answer to your question: The easiest way to convince people you are my bondmate is for me to touch you. Even something as simple as this will suffice.”

Understanding dawns. “When we were walking over here and you put your arm around me… that was for show? To convince them we are a mated pair?”

“While it did serve that purpose, it was not my primary motivation.”

“Oh?” I ask, unsure how to respond as his glowing green eyes stare deep into mine.

“I wanted to protect you, Elena.”

Something about his answer fills my heart with warmth. He’s the first person I’ve met since I woke up in this godforsaken nightmare who’s been kind to me.

I still don't understand why Vanek would do this for me, but I'm not going to question it anymore either.

"We should shower and rest," Vanek says. "We do not know when we will have the opportunity after this."

He's right. I move to the door across the way and it whooshes open to reveal a small cleansing room. There's only enough space for one person to move around in here, but at least it has a shower, a toilet, and a sink.

It's very sparse, but I don't care. When Vanek shows me how to activate the hot water, I can hardly wait to shower. It's been so long since I've bathed. Usually the masters would simply wave the ion wand over my body to clean me. It works, but it definitely is not the same.

Vanek leaves the room, and I immediately peel out of my clothes and step into the shower. The warm water flows over my shoulders and down my body, soothing away the tension in my muscles.

When I finish, I realize there are no fresh clothes to change into. So I grab the long, white towel and wrap it around myself. I open the door and a puff of steam escapes into the room as I step through.

Vanek's eyes widen when he turns to me. His cheeks and the tips of his ears turn a light shade of green as his gaze travels over my form.

CHAPTER 10

VANEK

Elena steps out of the cleansing room wearing nothing but a towel. My heart stutters and stops in my chest when I see her. Her wet hair cascades down her back and shoulders. The material of the towel hangs just above her knees, only covering her torso and thighs.

My mouth drifts open. Warmth fills my entire body, and I swallow thickly as I study her. She is the most beautiful female I have ever seen.

"Vanek?"

I quickly snap my jaw shut. "Yes?"

"Are they going to bring us more clothing?"

"I—" I start but stop. "They should," he replies. "But it may not be until tomorrow."

"Are you going to shower?"

Quickly, I nod then move into the cleansing room. As soon as the door shuts between us, worry spikes through me. I shower as fast as I can, concerned someone may come into the room while I'm in here. I do not like the idea of being separated from her, even for a moment. This place is crawling with all sorts of unsavory characters who, I have no doubt, would harm her, given the chance.

When I'm done showering, I grab a towel from the sink counter and wrap it loosely around my hips before stepping back into the room.

It does not escape my attention how Elena's eyes move over my form. Her cheeks flush a lovely shade of pink before she averts her gaze. Perhaps she is as attracted to me as I am to her.

The chime of the door startles us both. Lightning fast, I place myself between her and the door as it slides open. I stand protectively in front of her as Chylan steps in.

I narrow my eyes at the Patiko when he ushers two others in with trays of food and drink.

"Easy, V'loryn." He holds his feathered hands up in a placating gesture. "I am not going to harm your mate."

I snarl in response. "We need clothes. Now."

He nods, then snaps his fingers at one of the servers. They quickly exit and return with two pairs of nondescript pants and tunics.

When they are finished, they quickly leave.

As I hand Elena the clothing, she frowns. "They are afraid of you. Why? We're both slaves. It's not like we can harm them with these collars on."

"My species is one of the strongest and fastest," I explain. "They know that, if I chose, I would be able to kill at least two, perhaps three of them, before the collar could take me down."

"How do you know this?"

"Because I've done it before when I was captured." I pause. "I killed three Anguis masters before the collar completely immobilized me." He pauses. "It happened when I was in the V'loryn Defense Force. I was ambushed while on leave at one of the stations along the outer rim. Fortunately, my team rescued me less than an hour later."

Her jaw drops, but she quickly snaps it shut.

I hand her the clothes and turn my back preemptively, because I do not want to be separated from her while she changes, but I also do not want to make her uncomfortable.

A soft rustle of clothing behind me tells me she is changing. I have already resolved that I will not take her as my bondmate, but my body does not agree with this. It responds as though she were already mine. Everything within me longs to claim her, and seal her to me.

But I know that I cannot. I vowed long ago I would never take a mate.

Besides... I will not survive the Great Hunt anyway. Only one will leave the arena alive, and I will do everything in my power to make certain it is her.

CHAPTER 11

ELENA

When Vanek insists that I sleep in the bed and he'll stay on the floor, I refuse. "It's all right. We can share the bed."

His cheeks and the tips of his ears flush light green again as he nods. I lie down beneath the covers, and he crawls in beside me. I slept next to him last night, but that was different. Last night I was leaning against him, not lying down.

I'm not worried that he'll try anything, it's just... awkward, because he's attractive.

Sighing heavily, I force these errant thoughts away. I need to focus; I can't afford to be distracted.

He lies on his back beside me and I do the same; each of us staring up at the ceiling overhead.

I close my eyes, but it's no use. I'm too anxious to sleep, especially since I only have a vague idea of what to expect tomorrow. My mind begins to replay everything Vanek has told me about the Great Hunt.

The thing that keeps running through my mind is the fact

that it's not just the Hunters who could potentially be after us. The other players could be, too, because they want to eliminate their competition and increase their chances of winning.

I turn onto my side, toward Vanek. He turns to me as well, his glowing green eyes studying me curiously.

"You said other players could try to harm us."

He nods.

"What if we form an alliance with someone else? Then we could watch out for each other... strength in numbers and all that."

His brow creases into a frown. "I do not know that we could trust anyone else."

"What about the Lycaon who was in the cell beside us?"

His frown deepens. "His kind are savage and unpredictable."

"He had some bad things to say about you, too," I point out.

Vanek lowers his gaze, a contemplative look on his face. "I am not sure I would trust him enough to form an alliance."

"What about someone else?... Anyone?" I ask.

"No one. The only people we can trust are mine and, potentially, the Mosaurans."

My brows shoot up. "The Mosaurans? The dragon people?" I ask, thinking back on the few I saw in the gladiator rings. The two I saw had silver scales, reptilian eyes, and leathery wings. "They're... friends of yours?"

A hint of a smile ghosts his lips. "Hard to believe, is it not?"

I laugh. "Yeah, it is."

"We recently formed an alliance with them. They are a warrior race and can be... aggressive, but they are honorable." He pauses. "We also have an alliance with the Aerilon."

I think back on the few Aerilon I've seen. They were

beautiful, reminding me of stories I'd read as a child about the Fae with their clear, dragon-fly-esque membranous wings.

Vanek continues. "I did not notice any V'loryns, Mosaurans, or Aerilon in the crowd today, but I do not doubt there will be a few of them in the Great Hunt."

"Why is that?"

"Because Hunters pay thousands of credits to hunt their kind. Especially Mosaurans and V'loryns. *We* are a challenge. The Mosaurans because of their strength and ability to shift into great winged beasts, and V'loryns because of our strength and our speed."

When he mentions those qualities, worry fills me. "About that," I hedge. "I'm worried that I'm going to slow you down… be a burden to you."

His glowing green eyes meet mine evenly. "Do not think such things. You are not a burden."

I open my mouth to protest but decide it's probably best to keep it shut. I *am* a burden. Someone he's going to have to look out for. I know he is aware of this. The fact that he denies it only confirms that he's a good person who actually cares.

As I lie next to him, I can't help but think how blessed I am to have found him. He's intelligent, kind, caring, and devastatingly handsome… I know he said touch is forbidden, but if we're supposed to convince people we're mated, it can't be avoided anyway.

I reach out and take his hand, threading my fingers through his. "I know you said you'll keep me safe, but I want you to know it goes both ways. I'll do everything I can to watch your back as well. I may not be as fast or as strong as you, but I'm not completely helpless. I had survival and combat training."

Gently, he squeezes my hand in return. "Thank you,

Elena," he replies softly. He studies me a moment. "Are you certain you are comfortable sharing the bed? I do not mind sleeping on the floor."

His concern touches me. "I trust you, Vanek. I know you wouldn't hurt me."

"Never," he murmurs.

"I know your people don't normally touch strangers, but —" I stop short, not sure how to ask what I want to ask.

"What is it?" He gives me a curious look.

It sounds pathetic, in my mind, but right now I don't care. I could die tomorrow. Why not enjoy the few moments of peace we have before we get dropped into some arena where we have to fight for our survival?

"Can you hold me?"

He blinks several times, obviously shocked by my request. I move quickly to add, "Just to sleep. Nothing else."

"Of course," he replies.

I move closer. He wraps his arms around me and I nestle into his chest, enjoying the warmth and safety of his embrace. "Goodnight," I whisper softly.

"Goodnight," he murmurs into my hair as I allow myself to fall away into sleep.

CHAPTER 12

VANEK

That she trusts me this much is something I had not anticipated would happen so quickly.

As she sleeps, I cannot help but watch her. She truly is more beautiful than anyone I have ever seen.

I am honored by her trust and I vow to do all I can to keep her safe. My thoughts drift to the two pills in my pocket, and I curse myself for my addiction. I have no need of them yet, but I fear what will happen when they are gone.

I will be rendered useless as I go through withdrawal, and she will be vulnerable to anyone who desires to harm her.

I know I should tell her about my addiction, but I cannot push the words past my lips. I don't want to see the fear and worry in her eyes that I might be unable to protect her.

The Lycaon's words resurface. He offered to be an ally, but I do not know if I trust him enough. I never thought there would be a time where I would pray to see a Mosauran, but I do now.

They may be a warrior race, but I know they are a people

of honor, first and foremost. And their ability to shift into their *draken* forms would ensure they could protect Elena from others.

I did not see any Mosaurans in the crowd today, but I am hopeful there will be at least one in the arena with us. If there is, I must find a way to approach him, and ask for an alliance.

Elena's life may depend upon it.

CHAPTER 13

ELENA

I wake to the sound of a growl nearby. My eyes snap open to find Vanek at the edge of the bed, facing the door to our room and crouched in a defensive position with his nails extended into lethal claws.

"I am here to collect your mate to get her ready for the Great Hunt, not to harm her." I recognize Chylan's voice right away. "Calm yourself and allow me to do my job."

"She does not leave my sight," Vanek snarls. "You can ready her here."

"I am afraid that is not how this works," the Patiko replies, not bothering to hide the irritation in his tone. "Now, move aside."

Vanek stands his ground.

Chylan sighs and gestures to one of the Craven behind him.

Without warning, Vanek's body arcs back. An angry roar rips from his throat, and he drops to his knees on the ground, his entire body shaking as they shock his collar repeatedly. Despite this, he struggles to remain upright, snarling and gnashing his fangs.

"Stop!" I cry out, leaping from the bed and rushing to his side. "I'll go with you. Just leave him alone."

The Craven nods and Vanek collapses to the floor, panting heavily.

Panic fills me. I take his hand. "Vanek, are you—"

Time slows and stops as emotions rush toward me like a giant wave crashing onto the shore of my mind as we form a connection through the bare touch of our skin. Devotion so intense it steals the breath from my lungs, expands, and fills my thoughts as his consciousness wraps thickly around my own like a warm and soothing comforter.

In this moment, any and all doubt has been entirely erased. Vanek would fight for me, die for me, kill to keep me safe. There is nothing he would not sacrifice to protect me.

Tears sting my eyes as they meet his, understanding passing between us.

Without warning, a barrier drops into place between us—his mental transference shield—pushing me back from the connection. I've done nothing to deserve his devotion, and I cannot bear him suffering for me. I reach down and cup his cheek. "I don't want you to be hurt because of me," I whisper.

His expression remains impassive, but I do not miss the tears glossing his eyes.

"I'll be fine, Vanek." I speak softly. "We don't have a choice."

I start to pull away, but he grips my hand firmly. *"No!"* The word arcs through me like lightning, and I realize it's him speaking in my mind.

In all the time I've been a slave, no one has cared for me like this. My heart clenches, and I run my fingers through his hair, brushing it back from his handsome face. *"Please, don't fight them. Not now."* I try my hand at replying with my mind. *"There are too many of them. I don't want you to be hurt."*

He clenches his jaw and gives me a subtle nod.

I stand and face the Patiko. "I'm ready."

Another Patiko moves in the doorway. "I have come for the V'loryn male," he says chipperly.

The smile slips from his expression as soon as he notices Vanek on the floor. "What have you done to him?" He casts an accusatory glance at Chylan.

Chylan shrugs. "He was being aggressive."

"Of course, he was," the other retorts. "You were trying to separate him from his mate. You know how possessive V'loryn males are of their females." He sighs. "We cannot have him agitated like this before they are presented. This will not do at all." He tsks.

He walks over to Vanek. "I am Triran. Do not fret. I will ensure your mate is never more than a room away from you. How does that sound?"

Vanek studies him. His gaze sweeps to me, and I dip my chin in agreement. "That is acceptable," Vanek finally replies.

Vanek stands, and together, we follow the two Patikos out into the hallway.

CHAPTER 14

VANEK

When the new Patiko speaks to me, I realize this is the best offer I am going to receive under the circumstances. It is either accept or fight and end up dead. I would be able to take out at least two or three of them before being brought down, but then Elena would be left alone to face the Hunt.

No. I must survive long enough to ensure she is the last one standing. I must make sure she wins and is granted her freedom.

As we walk down the hallway, several others pass us by, each of them led by a slaver and another person assigned to ready them for the presentation before being sent off to the Great Hunt.

I observe as Chylan leads Elena into a room beside mine. My eyes remain locked onto her form until she is ushered inside. When the door seals shut behind her, anger floods my veins. A deep growl rumbles in my chest.

Triran turns to me, blinking rapidly. His gaze shifts to the

Craven behind me, and he gestures to the door. "Leave us so I may work."

The Craven straightens. "Are you sure you wish to be alone with him? He might kill you."

Triran looks back at me, and I do not miss the worry that flits briefly across his expression before he replies, "No, he will not."

"It's your life," the Craven says before stepping back out into the hallway.

I level an icy glare at the Patiko, and he sighs heavily. "If you kill me, they will separate you from her for sure. Is that what you want?"

I narrow my eyes. "No," I reply, unable to hide the anger in my voice. "You know I do not."

The room is about twice the size of the bedroom we slept in last night. There is a table with clothing already laid out upon it, a large mirror across the way, and a changing room divider nearby.

He gestures to the clothes. "Try these on."

Reluctantly, I move to the table and pick up the fabric. I'm surprised to find it is military grade material. I step behind the changing divider and quickly dress. The material fits like a second skin, and yet, it is not uncomfortable in the slightest.

When I step out from behind the divider, Triran's eyes light up. "Absolutely stunning. Fierce and handsome and lethal," he practically purrs. "You will definitely be a crowd favorite."

He turns back to the table, and I notice another piece of material lying atop that was not there before. He gathers it and brings it over to me. He darts a glance around the room before unfolding the fabric. "This is something I believe your mate will appreciate," he says in a low voice.

I inhale sharply when I notice the small blade nestled in the middle of the fabric. My eyes snap up to his.

"I know what she is," he whispers. "Her people have no natural defenses. No claws, fangs, wings, or venom. This is the best I could do on short notice."

I open my mouth to speak, but he continues. "I know you hate my brother—Chylan—right now, but please do not kill him. It is all an act, you know. He wasn't actually going to let her be rented out to clients at the pleasure house. We have others set up there to pretend to be clients. They would have pretended she was hurt during… unspeakable acts and would have offered generous compensation to your masters to buy her."

My head jerks back.

"It is the only way slavers will part with a female they intend to place in the Great Hunt."

"Why are you doing this?" I ask, instantly suspicious, wondering if this is some sort of test, if I'm being watched. "Why help us?"

"My sister was stolen from our village and sold to slavers," he says. "By the time we found her, it was too late. The male who killed her is here. He is the one hosting the Hunt this cycle. We came here to get close enough to disrupt the Hunt and kill him."

He says the last words with such rage in his eyes, I believe he speaks truth.

"Listen carefully. There are four areas: each of them a varied climate. You must make your way to the one of ice and snow. My people will find you there, and we will get you out."

"I do not understand. Why us and not someone else?"

"Because you are the ones who were assigned to Chylan and me." He swallows thickly as sadness reflects behind his eyes. "We would save everyone if we could, but it is not possible. Not yet, anyway. Even if we cannot save everyone, my brother and I would save the ones we can. Do you understand?"

"Yes," I reply solemnly. "I do. You must contact my people. They will help you."

"Your people will not believe me." He scoffs.

"How do you know?"

"I've tried." He huffs. "Several times. Your emperor did not care."

Everything falls into place. "You are speaking of Emperor Zotal."

"Yes," he replies sharply. "Who else?"

"Zotal is no longer emperor. He was deposed. Emperor Kalvar is a wise and just leader. He will aid you. I am certain of it."

"How do you know this?"

I straighten. "Because I am T'Hale Vanek of the Great House A'msir—one of the seven ruling Houses of V'lora."

"You are nobility?" He blinks several times. "How in the stars were you caught?"

I sigh heavily as frustration burns through me. "Our ship was sabotaged by slavers." I pause, not wanting to ask this, but I must. "Do you have any neural relaxers? I… am in need of some to avoid withdrawal."

His head jerks back. "They are highly addictive. Why were you taking those in the first place?"

"Why does anyone?" I reply, unable to hide the bitter tinge to my voice. "To forget something I'd rather not remember."

He stops short and his mouth drifts open. "I know who you are."

His gaze holds mine as he studies me. "Your name. I have heard it before. You are the V'loryn Lord who found the missing Aerilon Princess. You returned her body to her home world."

I close my eyes as the dark memories flow through me. Curling my hands into fists at my side, I struggle to push them back down. I was too late to save her and, even though it was many cycles ago, I have never forgiven myself for it. "How did you hear of this?"

He arches a feathered brow. "It is not often one hears of a V'loryn doing anything for someone other than their own kind."

Clenching my jaw, I change the subject. "I have been weaning myself off the relaxers, but I still have need of them."

"You will need some before they drop you in the Hunt. Otherwise, you will go through withdrawals."

"I am aware," I reply, unable to hide the slight irritation in my tone as he points out the obvious. "Can you procure any for me?"

"I will try my best, but I cannot promise anything."

"Thank you."

"Now, tell me," he says, leaning a bit closer. "How do I contact your people?"

After I give him detailed instructions, he gives me a skeptical look. "What if they do not believe me?"

"Ask to speak to T'Hale Marek—the emperor's nephew. His mate is Terran. Tell him you have found one of her people. He will grant you an audience."

The Patiko nods. "I will do this. And I will pray that my request for help will not fall upon deaf ears again."

"It will not," I reassure him.

"We shall see," he replies, not bothering to hide the doubt in his voice. "Either way, my brother and I will help you escape with your mate. But remember, you must make it to the part of the arena with ice and snow. It is the only place we can hide a cloaked vessel."

"Understood."

He gestures to me. "You are ready for the presentation. I suspect your mate is, as well." He motions to the door. "Let us go." He adds. "You *must* convince everyone she is yours and that you will die without her."

"Why?"

"When they take you to the arena, they will be less likely to separate you if they believe it will displease the crowd."

My mouth drifts open. "I thought they would keep us together for sure since we are mated."

He shakes his head. "Not necessarily. Only pressure from the crowd will motivate them to drop you together into the arena. I have seen them separate mates before."

Worry tightens my chest, but I force it back down. I cannot bear the thought of Elena being alone in the arena. Anything could happen to her while I try to locate her.

Anger floods my system. I will kill anyone who tries to separate us. I swear it to the stars.

CHAPTER 15

ELENA

I'm silent as I stand before the full-length mirror, assessing my outfit. The material is black and soft as silk. It's tailored perfectly to my body, like wearing a second skin. Chylan stands behind me, twisting my hair into a long braid that hangs down my back.

I keep my eyes trained on his reflection, watching him warily.

When he's finished, he places his hands on my shoulders and turns me to face him. I recoil instinctively and something akin to sadness flashes behind his eyes. "I want you to know something."

"What?" I ask, studying him with a cautious look.

"I only suggested the pleasure house so I could get you out of the Hunt."

My head jerks back. "What?"

"My brother, Triran, and I, we are part of the resistance trying to put an end to the Great Hunt. We had an agent ready to intercept you in the Pleasure House. He was going to buy your freedom from your Master."

"I—" I start but stop, unsure if I can trust his words.

He continues. "I can sense your hesitance to trust me, and I do not blame you. We do not have much time, so I will speak fast."

He darts a glance around the room, verifying we are, in fact, alone. Once he's satisfied, he begins. "Once we leave here, you and your mate will be taken to the transport to head for the arena. The crowd will be watching your every move. You must convince them you are a mated pair, even if you are not." He arches a knowing brow. "If you become a crowd favorite, the Hunters will be less likely to separate you from him when they drop you over the arena."

"I thought they would keep us together for sure."

"Not necessarily," he says.

Panic spikes through me, but I force myself to calm as he continues.

"Each contestant is dropped at a different location to begin the Hunt. The goal is to spread you all out and make the Hunt more challenging. Many times, however, in the past, they have opted to keep mated pairs together." He pauses. "You must take out your tracker as soon as possible, then make your way to the mountain of ice and snow. We will get you out there."

My mind begins to spin with this information, dozens of questions sit on the tip of my tongue. Before I can ask, however, the chime of the door startles us both.

Chylan leans in and claps a hand on my shoulder. "Do whatever you must to survive. Make it to the mountain, and we will find you there."

"And if I can't?"

He frowns. "Then try to survive. Only the winner makes it out of the Hunt alive."

I inhale sharply.

Vanek never mentioned this.

He made it sound like both of us were going to make it to the end. I shake my head, wondering if I've heard him wrong. "Only one? You're certain?"

"Yes. It is this way with each Great Hunt."

"Enter!" he calls out.

A Craven steps in and looks at me. "It is time."

When we walk out of the room, and into the hallway, Vanek is already there with Triran. He is dressed in a black outfit, matching mine. The material fits like a second skin on us both, hiding nothing of his lean, muscular form beneath.

No one else is around as he leans close and whispers. "Take this."

He places a knife in my hand. My eyes widen, but I quickly tuck it into my boot.

He dips his chin then holds his arm out to me. I loop mine through his. We are supposed to be presenting ourselves as a couple, or "mated pair" as the Patiko said.

I would prefer to hold onto him anyway, but this way I have an excuse.

We make our way through the building, passing several other contestants along the way, each of them eyeing us with a look akin to envy, if I'm not mistaken.

I lean closer to Vanek and whisper. "Why are they looking at us like they're mad?"

"Because couples have an advantage in the arena. With two of us, we can watch over one another without fear of being betrayed. Whereas, any alliances they make might end in their demise."

As we walk side by side, I notice the Lycaon from our ship being led by another Craven in front of us.

We stop before a large set of double doors. The dull roar of the crowd outside is already near deafening. A bead of sweat trickles down my spine and my hands begin trembling involuntarily while we wait for them to open. "What happens now?" I ask Vanek.

"We are to be paraded before the crowd as we walk to the transport. From there we will be taken to the arena."

He turns to me, worry reflecting in his eyes, despite his impassive gaze. "I will protect you, Elena. My vow."

Before I can respond, the door swings wide open. The roar of the crowd so loud it nearly drowns out the announcer's voice when he calls out each contestant's name as they are led to the transport.

When the Lycaon steps out, I overhear his name is Ryker.

They announce Vanek and me as a mated pair and the crowd goes absolutely mad, their shout and cries even louder than they were before. Vanek responds by wrapping a protective arm around my waist, pulling me close.

I know we're technically only doing this for show, but I can't deny that it comforts me. I'm scared, but I know, if not for Vanek by my side, I'd be absolutely terrified. I know nothing of this world beyond what I've seen as a slave, whereas, he is familiar with most of these other alien species and has some idea of what we're about to face.

He helps me up onto the transport and they strap us into the seats.

Another Craven walks up to us. "Hold your arm out for your tracker."

Vanek extends his arm, and I watch the Craven press a strange metal instrument to his skin. He depresses a button and Vanek levels an icy glare at him before he moves on to me.

The Craven snarls as he grabs my arm roughly. I try to twist away, but it's no use. His vise-like grip holds me in place as he presses the metal instrument to my skin.

A harsh click sounds as pain shoots into my forearm. A

scream rips from my throat when intense heat blooms from the site, burning through my flesh like fire. He releases my arm and I hold it tight to my chest, gritting my teeth against the pain.

Vanek's eyes meet mine, full of concern. "Elena, are you all right?"

Shakily, I nod. It's a lie though. I am anything but all right at this moment.

I remember Triran's instructions. We have to find a way to remove these trackers as soon as possible.

After everyone is inside and their trackers have been placed, the engines begin to spin up. The soft hum reverberates through the hull as we lift off. The windows across the way are small and too high for me to see anything. Vanek, however, tips his chin up to get a better look—several of the others doing the same, including Ryken.

As I scan the rows across from us, I search for any Aerilon or Mosaurans in the crowd.

Hope sparks inside me when I notice a Mosauran in the far corner.

As if sensing my gaze upon him, the Mosauran's silver eyes snap to mine. He is covered from head to toe in silver-white scales.

His leathery wings are tucked back against his side.

I lean closer to Vanek. "Didn't you say your people are allies with theirs?"

He nods.

"Then maybe we should approach him about an alliance in the arena."

Vanek nods. "We will search for him when we land."

Small hover cameras float around us, pausing at each contestant before moving on. I assume it's for the audience that watched us depart earlier.

One of the handlers unfastens the seat strap of the Anguis

across the way and pulls him to his feet. He presses a small disc to his back and walks him to the center of the transport.

A hatch opens directly in the center, and my jaw drops as I watch the Craven push the Anguis out the opening.

A parachute opens from the small disc when he falls away, and my heart begins hammering wildly in my chest. I've never been good with heights. I turn to Vanek, unable to hide the panic in my voice. "That's how they're going to send us to the arena?"

I'd thought when he referred to us being dropped, that it meant they were simply going to land and let us off at a specific location.

He nods. He rests his hand atop mine and squeezes it reassuringly. "I will be with you. They will send us out together. It will be fine."

Shakily, I nod.

My fear increases exponentially as, one by one, each contestant is pushed through the opening. Some of them are even dragged kicking and screaming before being thrown from the transport.

When it's my turn, one of the Craven steps forward. He unfastens my seat strap and grips my forearm, jerking me to my feet. I glance back at Vanek, waiting for them to get him, as well. Instead, the Craven begins marching me to the opening.

"Wait!" Vanek calls out. "I am supposed to go with her!"

"Not this time," the Craven replies. "The crowd wants to see you work to find your precious mate."

CHAPTER 16

VANEK

Panic spikes through me as the Craven leads Elena toward the opening. "Wait!" I cry out. "You cannot do this!"

He flashes a sinister snarl as Elena fights against his hold.

I extend my nails into claws, tearing at the strap binding me to my seat, but it's no use. I cannot slice through it.

Elena manages to break free. She rushes back to me, frantically fumbling with the strap, but it is coded and will not release.

Tears brighten her eyes, but she blinks them back as she spins and kicks out at the Craven when he tries to grab her again.

An angry roar rips from my throat when he lunges for her. "Do not touch her!"

He hits her with the shock stick, and she crumples to the floor. He takes advantage of her momentary stun and scoops her in his arms.

"Elena!"

"Vanek!" she cries out as he drags her to the opening.

Her eyes lock onto mine and a terrified scream rips from her throat as he throws her through the opening.

I roar in anger, thrashing against my bindings so hard the metal of my seat begins to warp and fold.

The Craven ignores me and frees the Lycaon next. Ryker's eyes snap to mine.

Lightning fast, he rips the shock stick from the Craven's belt and hits him with it, full force.

The Craven cries out a moment before crumpling to the floor in a boneless heap. I watch as the Lycaon drags him over to my seat and presses his hand to the scan code, freeing me. He slaps a chute chip on my back.

"Go!" Ryker yells. "Find your mate!"

Without hesitation, I jump up and race for the opening. Desperation claws at my chest as I begin to fall.

Scanning the area below me, I make a mental note of the four regions of the arena, then search the skies for Elena.

I see her falling toward the forested area several clicks from me. "Elena!" I cry out, but she cannot hear me.

My heart pounds as I watch her disappear below the tree line and out of view. I make a mental note of her location. As soon as I land, I must find her. Quickly. Before the Hunters do.

CHAPTER 17

ELENA

I tumble through the air in a complete and terrifying freefall a moment before my chute snaps open, slowing my descent. My heart hammers in my chest as I scan the area beneath me.

Tall trees, similar to pine trees on Terra, but with red needles instead of green, blanket the landscape, their canopy so thick, I can't see through it to the ground. I brace myself as they rise up to meet me.

Panic floods my system as I descend. I tense as my boots scrape the tops of the trees and I crash through the branches, holding my hands out in front of me to avoid them hitting my face.

A choked scream escapes me when I jerk to a halt. The wires of my chute snag and tangle in the leaves and branches, leaving me dangling high above the ground below.

I squeeze my eyes shut as a wave of nausea and dizziness rolls through me. My pulse pounds in my ears at the struggle to calm myself. I know I shouldn't be so terrified of heights.

After all, I got my pilot's license and used to fly ships. But I've also never been hanging from a tree this far off the ground before either.

I wrap my arms and legs around the closest branch. My entire body is trembling and sweat slicks my palms as I carefully pull the knife from my boot. I grip it firmly, afraid I'll lose it. Drawing in a deep breath, I start cutting at the wires to free myself.

The sound of voices carries on the wind, and I still, listening to try to determine which direction they're coming from.

"I saw her drop over here," one of them says.

Ice fills my veins as the sounds of booted steps crashing through the thicket below grow closer.

Indecision wars within me, and I'm not sure if I should keep cutting to try to free myself or remain still. Panic twists deep inside me as two Craven come into view below me.

Each of them are fully equipped with blaster rifles and other weapons strapped to their belts and chests. They must be Hunters, because contestants weren't given anything for defense.

"Up there!" the first one points, his yellow cat-like eyes practically glittering with hunger.

The second one looks to him. "Do you want the first kill?"

"Thank you," he replies. "I will give you first shot at the next one."

Unable to free myself or hide, I'm easy prey up here. Fear grips my heart in an iron vise as I frantically begin sawing at the wires again with my blade.

A thunderous roar fills the air, and they both spin toward the sound. A flash of movement races through the trees with inhuman speed. Hope sparks in my chest as I recognize Vanek barreling straight toward them.

His eyes are feral, obsidian black, and his fangs are fully

extended. He slices out with lethal claws, ripping the throat out of the first one.

Obsidian blood sprays out as the Craven grasps at his neck and drops to his knees. He opens his mouth to speak, but only a choked gurgling sound escapes before he collapses in a pool of blood.

The second one aims his blaster at Vanek but too late. Vanek grabs the barrel and rips it from his grasp with one hand, stabbing his claws deep in the Craven's chest with a sickening squelch.

The Craven falls forward and goes still.

Vanek lifts his gaze to me, and my heart stops. Covered in blood and with his fangs and claws fully extended, he is the image of every nightmare I ever had of Vampires when I was a child.

But this is Vanek, and I'm not afraid of him.

"I'm going to get you down, Elena!"

His eyes swirl from black to their normally glowing green as he scales the trees. He uses his claws to slice away the last of the wires and pulls me to him. "Hold on to me," he says as he shifts me so I'm on his back.

Wrapping my arms around his neck and my legs around his waist, I squeeze my eyes shut as he climbs down. I'm too terrified to look for fear I'll get nauseated again.

As soon as we reach the ground, he carefully slides me off his back. "We have to remove the trackers, then we must hide."

Numbly, I nod, too terrified to speak; worried more Hunters might be nearby.

He takes the blade from me and holds out my arm. "Brace yourself. This will hurt," he says, not bothering to mince words.

Carefully, he slices a small line down my forearm. I grit my teeth against the pain when he uses the blade to scoop out the tracker just beneath the skin. Bile rises in my throat, but I swallow it back as it pops free.

Once he's done with me, he wastes no time digging into his own arm and removing his tracker.

He moves to the Hunters and rips a strip of fabric from their clothing. Quickly, he binds it around my arm. When he starts to rifle through their supplies, I ask. "What about your arm? Don't you need to—"

"My kind heal quickly," he says, not bothering to look up from his task of searching their bodies and belongings. He grabs their packs and blaster rifles and turns to me. "Do you know how to use this?"

I shake my head.

He hands it to me and points to a panel on the side. "Depress this to fire. Do not hesitate. Understand?"

"Y-yes."

He loops both packs so they rest on his front and gestures for me to climb onto his back. When I hesitate, he adds, "Your weight is nothing to me. V'loryns possess two to three times the strength of Terrans. It will be faster if I carry you."

He kneels, and I climb onto his back. Without warning, he lurches forward and begins to race through the forest with lightning speed.

Trees blur past as he rushes through the dense bramble like it were nothing but a mere inconvenience to him. We travel for what feels like forever before he finally slows and tips up his chin, nostrils flaring.

"What is it?"

"There is water nearby." He gestures up ahead. "That way."

We continue on, but a bit slower now. He stops every so often, training his ears in each direction, listening for any sounds of pursuit.

When he is satisfied there are none, we continue until we reach a waterfall.

The heavy curtain of water falls over the mountain above, spilling into a large pool below.

"We should wash our wounds, so that the scent of our blood will not be carried on the wind, attracting Hunters or predators."

I glance down at my clothes and the several crimson stains from where I bled. I notice the dark stains on Vanek as well from his bleeding. Vanek follows my gaze and then scans the forest around us. "We will have to wash our clothing as well."

He removes his tunic and when he starts to unfasten his pants, my cheeks flare bright red and I avert my gaze.

He goes still. "If you wish to bathe first, I will turn my back."

I lift my eyes to him. My gaze travels over the hard planes of muscle that line his abdomen and chest. He is the image of masculine perfection made manifest before me. My mouth drifts open, but I quickly snap it shut.

I'm an adult. It's ridiculous to be embarrassed about changing in front of this gorgeous man.

He mistakes my nervousness for fear. Sadness reflects in his gaze. "I vow that I will not touch you against your will, Elena."

"I know you won't, Vanek. I'm just... embarrassed," I admit. "I trust you."

A hint of a smile crests his lips. "I am honored by your trust."

An idea occurs to me. "How about I get in the water first, and then I'll turn my back so you can as well?"

He cocks his head to the side as if contemplating my suggestion before he nods. "An excellent solution."

CHAPTER 18

VANEK

It seems my Si'an T'kara is shy about her body, but so are my people. We never go out in public unclothed, unlike some of the other races.

I scent the air again, but detect no one else nearby.

I listen to the soft rustle of her clothing, and my heart begins to pound as I hear her entering the water. Although I know that I should be concentrating on other things, I cannot stop thinking about the fact that she is unclothed behind me.

She releases a strange sound of distress, and I spin to face her. "What is wrong?"

Before she can answer, my eyes widen as I take in her nearly nude form. Only a small band of fabric covers her breasts and a triangular scrap of fabric hides her pelvic area and backside.

She covers herself with her hands. "Turn around!"

I'm so mesmerized it takes me a moment to remember how to move, form words or even so much as a coherent thought. Finally, I force myself to turn my back to her. "Forgive me," I say quickly. "I thought you were in distress."

"I was," she says. "It's a bit cold in here."

It's on the tip of my tongue to suggest that I could share my body heat with her. It would be a rational choice if not for my desire. I am hesitant to place myself in a position that might make her afraid if my body responds to her nearness.

Already, my l'ok is erect and painfully engorged with want to join my body to hers. Even my knot is beginning to expand. Drawing in a deep breath, I try to force myself to calm, but it is no use.

Even though I have not claimed her as my mate, my body does not realize this. She is my Si'an T'kara, and I long more than anything to claim her.

"All right," she calls out. "I'll turn around so you can undress."

I unfasten my pants and then quickly make my way into the water, not wanting her to risk seeing how her mere presence affects me.

As I enter the river, my eyes trace over the delicate curve of her shoulders and the elegant column of her neck. She shivers slightly, and I want only to take her in my arms and hold her close, but I force myself to maintain my distance, not wanting to scare her.

"You can turn around now," I tell her.

She dips her head beneath the water to wash her hair, and I do the same. I am much taller than her, and while I am standing on the bottom of the riverbed, she is swimming nearby.

Thoughts of her drowning or being swept downriver fill my mind, and panic rushes through me at the mere idea of her in any danger.

"Please stay nearby," I tell her. "If you were to have a problem, I cannot swim."

She frowns. "You never learned to swim."

"In theory, I could probably tread water for a very short distance but it would be rather difficult. My people… our bodies are so dense, we are unable to effectively swim as yours do."

She floats closer to me, and I swallow thickly.

Without warning, she screeches out in alarm. She jumps up into my arms, climbing halfway up my body. "There's something in the water!"

Instantly, my fangs and claws descend, readying to defend her. I hold her close, scanning the water, and notice a nearby fish. Relief moves through me. "It is only a fish, Elena."

Her heart pounds against my chest as she pulls back just enough to meet my gaze. "You're sure?"

I glance at the small fish once more as it swims nearby. "Yes."

As I hold her close, my entire body flushes with warmth. I am acutely aware that only the thin scrap of material between her thighs separates us. Something dark and primal stirs deep within as my gaze drops to the curve of her neck and shoulder, locking onto the pulsing artery of her neck.

I long more than anything to sink my teeth deep into her flesh and seal her to me in the sacred blood ritual of the S'acris, claiming her as my mate.

But I know I cannot do this. Even if she wanted me, I could not take her as mine. I will not make anyone share my mind and the nightmares that plague me.

As I hold her, my nostrils flare as I note the delicate scent of her arousal. It seems I am not the only one affected by our close proximity.

I am loath to let her go. Her skin is petal-soft beneath my fingers and her scent is intoxicating. But I know that I cannot hold her forever. Even if I want to.

"Would you like me to put you down?"

CHAPTER 19

ELENA

With my arms around Vanek's neck and my legs around his waist, my entire body hums in awareness of his. His length is a hard bar between us, and after everything I've been through I'm surprised that instead of being nervous or afraid, desire pools deep inside me.

As his intense gaze holds mine, the warmth of his breath fans across my skin and he smells of cinnamon and warm spice. I drop my eyes to his lips, and I wonder what it would be like to kiss him… or if his people even kiss.

"Would you like me to put you down?"

My first inclination is to say no, but instead I force myself to nod *yes*.

As soon as he lowers my feet gently to the ground, I'm acutely aware that he is entirely naked. I turn around before I'm tempted to see what the rest of him looks like unclothed.

We quickly get dressed. Our clothes are already dry even

though they've just come out of the water. This material, whatever it is, is incredible.

Once we're dressed, Vanek lifts his gaze to the rock wall behind the falls. He turns so I can get on his back again before he walks around the edge of the water and toward the wall.

He follows a path behind the falls, and we find a network of openings—two of them large enough to enter.

"We can shelter in those caves," he says.

Effortlessly, he climbs up the rocks, hoisting us up onto the closest ledge. I climb off his back, and he pulls himself up to standing. His eyes narrow as he scans the interior. It's dimly lit, so I can't see much.

"Can you see anything?"

He nods. "My people are able to see almost as well in the dark as we can in the light. There is nothing in this cavern. It is safe."

He guides me inside, and we begin to go through the supply packs we found. A cool breeze blows through the cave and I shiver involuntarily. Despite my attempt to be calm, I'm still afraid we might have been followed here.

My every muscle is tense in anticipation of having to fight or run.

Vanek pulls out a blanket from each pack. He arranges one on the floor and drapes the other around my shoulders, taking care to make sure I'm wrapped completely to combat the chill.

After everything I've been through, just that extra bit of care makes tears spring to my eyes, but I somehow blink them back.

In the darkness, the glow of his green eyes accentuates the handsome lines of his face. His expression remains impassive, but something akin to sadness flashes briefly behind his eyes, and I don't understand why.

CHAPTER 20

VANEK

The acrid scent of her fear is thick in the cave. She is afraid of me, and rightly so. According to the Terrans I know, we remind them of monsters from their ancient Terran myths. Vampires, I believe they were called.

My best friend—Marek—his Terran Fated One was terrified when she first learned the truth.

Elena saw my claws and fangs before now, but this is the first time she witnessed me killing anyone, and I hate that it has made her afraid.

I make certain to keep some distance from her, not wanting to add to her distress. I want only to keep her safe and protect her. I had no choice but to kill those Hunters, but I cannot imagine how horrifying that must have been for her to witness.

When I saw the Hunters about to end her life, blinding rage consumed me. The need to end their lives, to protect what was mine, was all I could think of. I lost myself to the madness of bloodlust and, even now, I do not regret sating the monster inside me and making them pay for trying to harm my Si'an T'kara.

I observe as she eats only half of her nutrient bar and folds the wrapper over the remainder to save the other half, slipping it into a pocket on her tunic.

"Are you not hungry?"

She lowers her gaze. "I am, but I'm all right for now. I learned quickly in captivity to always save something for later whenever I could. The masters forgot to feed us several times."

My heart clenches. I cannot imagine all she has been through.

"Sometimes," she begins, "they would leave me in the pleasure simulators for… days. Only allowing me a few breaks here and there. Oftentimes, they'd forget to feed me." A tear slips down her cheek. "I was so afraid when Chylan suggested they send me to the pleasure house when we first arrived on the planet. But he was actually trying to help me escape," she says. "He and his brother, Triran, are part of a resistance."

"Triran explained this to me," I tell her. "He is also the one who gave me the blade to give to you."

Her eyes snap up to mine. "Did he tell you about their escape plan?"

"Yes. That is why we are headed toward the mountain in the snow terrain part of the arena. I figure we should reach it in the next few days if everything goes well."

"Do you believe them?"

"Yes, I do. They took great risk passing me the weapon to give to you. If they'd been caught, they would have likely been executed or thrown into the arena with us."

An angry roar sounds in the distance, and she stills, eyes

wide as she searches the darkness beyond the cave. "What was that?"

"Likely a Craven Hunter celebrating a kill."

Her gaze snaps to me, and I already know what she will ask, so I put her at ease. "We are safe in here. For now. I do not scent anyone else nearby."

"You can smell if someone is close?"

"You cannot?"

She shakes her head.

I did not know this about Terrans. But I do know they require more rest than my people. "You should sleep, Elena. I will stay awake and keep watch."

She nods, then lies down.

I turn my back to her to face the cave entrance, keeping my blaster trained on that area in case anyone dares try to catch us unaware. Reaching into my pocket, I pull out half a pill of my remaining two neural relaxers.

Half a pill won't put me to sleep, but it should be enough to still the tremors that have already begun in my hands.

I glance down at the small square—so deceptively-simple appearing—and shake my head softly.

I should never have started taking these.

At first, it was just to get some rest, but when I realized that they suppressed the nightmares of Al'ora's death, I started taking them more regularly, and before I realized it, I was addicted and could not sleep at all without them.

I place the half pill under my tongue and it dissolves almost instantly. I breathe a deep sigh of relief knowing the tremors will subside soon.

I train my ears toward Elena, listening for the sound of her breathing to become soft and even, indicating she is asleep. She trusts me to protect her, but it bothers me that she still fears me, in the same measure.

Then again, it must have been terrifying for her to see me kill those Hunters that way.

The sound of her teeth chattering draws my attention back to her, to find her shivering beneath the blanket.

I search for anything else in the supply bags to warm her but find nothing, so I lie down beside her with my back to her, the thick blanket between us. V'loryn body temperatures tend to run a bit warmer than that of Terrans. I only hope my proximity may help her.

I know she wanted me to hold her last night, but I doubt she wants me close to her now. Not after she witnessed me kill those Hunters.

I am not prepared when she snuggles against my back and wraps her arms around me. I go completely still, afraid to move and scare her. She presses the side of her face between my shoulders.

"You're so warm," she whispers against me.

My heart stops. "You are… not afraid of me?"

"No," she replies softly. "Why would you think that?"

Carefully, I turn in her arms to face her. "Because you watched me violently kill those Hunters." I pause. "I had no choice, Elena. I am sorry that it scared you. But know that I would never hurt you."

Her brown eyes study me a moment as if my words were absurd. "You saved me, Vanek. I'm not afraid of you."

I cannot deny that her words fill me with hope, but I ask again to be certain. "Even though I appear as a Vampire from your ancient Terran myths?"

A lovely smile crests her lips. "Actually… you look like an Elf, too. And from what I remember, they were the good guys in many of the stories I read."

I arch a brow. "Is that so?"

She nods. Her expression sobers. "Why are you helping me?"

"As I explained... my people have an alliance with yours. It is only natural that I should honor it."

"What you've done for me goes far beyond that," she says, and it's easy to read she is not convinced at hearing my abstraction.

I could tell her the truth of what she is to me. That she is my Si'an T'kara—my Fated One, but I realize it does not matter. My kind form a permanent mental link when we bond. That is simply something I can never do, especially to someone so rare and precious. I cannot even cope with my own nightmares; I could never ask another to carry them.

I will care for her, protect her, and keep her safe. I will do all I can to make sure she survives, no matter the cost to myself. And that will be enough... to know that she will survive.

Instead of telling her all of this, I offer another half-truth. "My people abhor slavery. In my time on the Defense Force, I saw enough of it to know I would do anything to help another escape a life of slavery. I understand it is not possible to save everyone, but it is important to save whomever we can."

"How do you live with it?" she asks softly. "How do you live with the things that you saw?"

"It is not easy," I admit. "I have nightmares... like you."

Her eyes snap up to mine, full of understanding. "Sometimes, I fight falling asleep," she says. "Because I worry that I'll have a nightmare about being in the pleasure simulator again." A tear slips down her cheek. "And when it happens, I can't tell what is the dream and what's real. When I wake up, I worry that I'm still there."

"The same happens to me," I offer.

"Does it get easier?"

I cannot lie to her when I am still haunted by my dark memories. "I am not a good person to ask."

Silence settles in the space between us a moment before she continues. "I worry about the others," she whispers. "The rest of my crew." Tears brighten her eyes, but she blinks them back. "I just hope they're all still alive out there somewhere."

"Our people, along with the Aerilon and the Mosaurans, are finding more Terrans each day. Perhaps some of your crew are among those who have already been found."

"I wonder how long I was in stasis, and if my family are still alive," her voice quavers. "My mother always told us it does no good to worry on the things you can do nothing about."

"Sound advice."

A wistful smile curls my lips. "My older sister was always such a worrier, you know. Emilia would fret over every little thing. She was planning her wedding when we last spoke. She was arguing with her fiancé Emmet over all the details, trying to make sure everything was perfect."

I nod. "My sister, L'Tana, is the same. She constantly worries about things. One time our t'sar became ill. Even though the Healer insisted N'Sara would recover, my sister was beside herself with worry."

Her small brow furrows. "What's a t'sar?"

"They are similar to Terran panthers, except much larger. Instead of fur, they are covered in obsidian scales that change color based on their environment."

Her mouth drifts open. "Like chameleons?"

"Yes."

"Are they dangerous?"

"They can be. But not N'Sara. We found her when she was just a kit."

"Was she wounded or something?"

"She was the runt of the litter; her mother had abandoned her. So we decided to take her home with us."

Elena smiles. "What did your parents think about you bringing home a dangerous animal?"

A smile quirks my lips. "We kept it secret for many weeks."

CHAPTER 21

ELENA

"Weeks? That's impressive."

He arches a brow, and I can't help but think how handsome he is when he does this. "My best friend, Marek, helped us keep our secret by providing us with dried fish." Amusement sparks his eyes. "He is a good friend. He risked the stark disapproval of both my parents and his uncle to help us."

I laugh softly. "So, how'd your parents finally figure it out?"

"N'Sara would often sleep with one of us, and one morning we couldn't find her." He pauses. "I assumed she was with L'Tana, but when we realized she was gone, we panicked. We knew our parents would greatly disapprove if they found out we'd been keeping her."

"So what happened then?" I ask, dying to hear the rest of the story.

"L'Tana and I decided we had no choice but to tell our parents. It was still early, so we quietly slipped into their chambers to wake them, only to find N'Sara curled up beside them as if she were supposed to be there."

My mouth falls open. "Oh my gosh, did your parents have a heart attack?"

A smile quirks his lips. "Almost. We tried to coax N'Sara from the bed with a snack without waking my parents. She immediately flipped over and plodded to the edge of the bed, shaking her body and moving her tail back and forth, preparing to pounce."

Softly biting my lower lip, I wait with bated breath to hear how this turned out.

"Just as she leaped toward me, our parents woke up and cried out like a wild katir as she pummeled me, pinning me to the floor. They thought a t'sar was attacking us and my father jumped into action.

"As soon as he realized N'Sara was licking my hand, he knew something was amiss. So, we explained everything to them." Mirth dances behind his eyes. "As we did, N'Sara curled up in Father's lap as if she had always been his pet."

I laugh softly. "Then what happened?"

"It was my mother who said we could keep her, so she stayed in the castle with us."

I straighten. "You live in a castle?"

"Yes. I am T'Hale of the Great House of A'msir—one of the seven Great Houses of V'lora," he answers as if it's the most normal thing in the world to be nobility.

"And do you still have N'Sara?"

He nods, and something akin to sadness flashes in his eyes. "She has been my father's constant companion since my mother died."

I meet his gaze evenly. "I'm sorry about your mother."

"Thank you," he replies solemnly. "My father has never fully recovered from her death. The fact that he survived it at all is rare among my species."

"What do you mean?"

"When we mate, it is for life. We create a permanent mental bond with our partners. Mated pairs link their minds in the *al'nara*—the mind link. When the connection is broken when one dies, the other usually succumbs shortly after from *L'talla*."

"What is L'talla?"

"Broken bond sickness."

"How did your father survive it?"

"My mother made him promise to try to be strong for us, since he would be all we had. We were only children when my mother died."

My heart clenches at the sadness reflected in his eyes. "Your father and sister must be so worried for you."

"Chylan was going to try to get a message to my best friend, Marek. I am sure they are already searching for me." He pauses. "When they find us, we will locate your family, Elena, and search for your missing crew."

The conviction in his voice fills me with hope—something I haven't had in a long time. "Thank you, Vanek."

A low howl sounds in the distance, and I still. "It is the Lycaon," he says. "Their voices can travel quite far."

I glance at the entrance to the cave. "Do you think we're safe here?"

"For now." He tips his head up, and his nostrils flare. "I still do not scent anyone nearby."

I blink several times. "I can't believe your sense of smell is that acute."

A smile quirks his lips. "Your Terran Healers—Doctors," he corrects, "were surprised about this as well. My friend Marek was able to determine his Terran mate, Elizabeth, was carrying their child when her scent changed. It was less than two weeks into her pregnancy."

My mouth drifts open. It seems that not only are our

people allies, but we're compatible enough to have children together. I can't deny a growing attraction to Vanek, and the thought that his people aren't averse to marrying mine is… something I hadn't really thought of until now.

My cheeks heat under the scrutiny of his gaze as he arches his brow again. "This surprises you."

Although he says this like a statement, I recognize the question. "Yes."

A smile quirks his lips. "It was a shock for my people, as well, to discover we are compatible without medical intervention."

"A good surprise?" I ask, curious to know. "Or a bad one?"

"Good, I believe." He pauses. "Although, as with anything, there are always some who oppose anything that is not considered… normal."

He's right.

Prejudice is a universal concept, it seems.

"Do you know what they're having?" I ask. "A boy or a girl?"

"A son," he replies. "They have asked me to be his godfather when he is born."

I smile. "So… I take it you like kids?"

Sadness flits briefly across his expression. "I always thought I wanted a family someday. But now… I know it cannot be."

"Why?"

I could lie to her; give her an excuse. But instead, I decide to be honest. "As I explained, my people form permanent mental bonds with their mates. The things I have seen… I live with those nightmares every day. I cannot allow anyone else to suffer them with me."

The pain in his eyes makes my heart clench. I cup his cheek. "What happened to you, Vanek? What do you see in your nightmares?"

He lowers his gaze. “I would rather not speak of it, if you do not mind.”

I hate that he shuts me out when I want to help him. But I also know better than to push him into something he doesn’t want to do. “All right,” I whisper. “But if you ever… want to talk about it, I’m here.”

His glowing green eyes study me a moment before he nods softly and changes the subject. “You should rest, Elena,” he murmurs. “We should leave here in the morning.”

He starts to get up, but I stop him. “Stay with me.”

“You are certain?” he asks.

I nod, and he responds by pulling the blanket up over us both. I nestle against him, and close my eyes as I fall away into oblivion.

CHAPTER 22

VANEK

When I close my eyes, I mean to only enter a light sleep, but the half-pill of the neural relaxer affects me more strongly than I expected. As my mind begins to drift toward the darkness of sleep, I consider that perhaps the dose is much stronger than what I am normally used to.

I fight against the urge to fall into the inky blackness awaiting me as a gentle hum fills the back of my mind. Suddenly, I am aware of a faint presence at the edge of my consciousness. As I study it, tangled emotions rush through me.

Panic. Fear. Sadness. Despair.

They each rush toward me, crashing against the shore of my mind like a giant wave, and I realize the onslaught is coming from Elena. But how is this possible?

I trace along the connection and my heart stutters and stops when I see her.

She is in a small, cramped cage, curled up in the corner and crying. My heart clenches, and I cautiously approach her. *"Elena, what is wrong?"*

She lifts her head to me, tears running down her face as myriad images flow around me like a river. Terrible, horrific pictures of the abuse she has endured.

Pain and sadness threaten to overwhelm me, and I realize it is not just my own in response to what I am seeing; it is hers.

I kneel and take her hand. *"Elena."*

"Where are we?" she asks softly.

The image changes and we are standing in the middle of the garden on my family's estate.

"We are connected in the al'nara*—the mind link."* I pause. *"These are my memories of my family's gardens on our estate."*

Worry fills me. I am afraid she will see the nightmares that plague me almost every night in my dreams, and I fight hard to partition them away from her consciousness.

The yellow sun is bright in the pale orange sky overhead as a cool wind whips through the gardens. Lush, green grass covers the entire space. We walk along the gravel pathway, following one of the nearby streams winding under and beside it. Various trees and flowering plants with bright purple, yellow, and red blossoms line the walkway, but it is the oralia flowers that are most beautiful with their vibrant red and white blooms.

"They look like Terran roses but much larger," she says, studying them closely. She reaches out and traces her fingers over one of the vibrant blooms and smiles brightly. *"I can actually feel them. How is this possible?"*

"Because you are drawing them from my memories."

Her eyes search mine, her long, chestnut hair blowing softly around her shoulders. I observe as she gently tucks a few stray tendrils behind the curved shell of her ears.

She leans down and picks one of the bright red blooms. She brings it to her nose and inhales deeply, smiling. *"It feels so real. I can even smell them."*

N'Sara walks toward us. I reach out my hand, and she gently bumps my palm with her muzzle before dipping her head in a request for me to pet her.

"N'Sara," Elena murmurs, having read my mind. She laughs as N'Sara flops over onto the ground, asking to have her belly scratched.

She laughs and warmth blooms in my chest, spreading throughout my entire body. I have never felt such joy as I do in this moment.

"Your home is beautiful, Vanek."

She smiles as she studies the rest of the gardens all around us. *"Your world is like a paradise."*

Sadness tightens my chest. *"These gardens are a mere shadow of our world that was lost—V'lorys-that-was. Most of V'lora is a desert of crimson sand."*

A figure hovers in the corner of my vision, and I lift my gaze to see who it is. My heart stops when I recognize the woman whose memory is burned in my mind. Her long silver-white hair blows gently on the breeze as her clear, membranous wings flutter softly behind her. Her violet skin pales and her eyes shine with sadness.

"Who is that woman?" Elena asks.

Using all my strength, I force away the vision of Al'ora, desperate to shield Elena from my nightmares, only to fall back into her own.

I see her being dragged, fighting with all her might as the masters strap her into the pod for the pleasure simulators. Her panic and fear threaten to overwhelm and paralyze me.

"Vanek, help me!" she cries out, her image blurring with Al'ora's. I take her hand and concentrate, pulling us out of the connection.

I blink several times as I awaken. Guilt overwhelms me. I had not meant to link with her. The *al'nara* is sacred—an act only meant to be shared between bondmates.

Elena's eyes are bright with tears.

"Forgive me. I should not have linked with you, Elena."

CHAPTER 23

ELENA

As I study Vanek, the memory of my strange dream resurfaces. It was so lucid and vivid. Sadness fills me as I recall images from the dream.

"Forgive me," Vanek says, pain in his eyes. "I should not have linked with you, Elena."

"Was that… the al'nara?"

Despite his impassive expression, guilt is easily read in his eyes. "Yes. Forgive me. I… my mental shields must have been lowered as I slept. When you touched me, it created the telepathic connection between us."

I inhale sharply. Despair fills me as I think on the images he must have seen of my time in the pleasure simulators and all the beatings I endured from the masters. "You saw… what happened to me?"

Tears sting my eyes at the painful memories.

I search his gaze, but instead of judgment, I find sympathy and understanding. He pulls me to his chest, holding me close.

The steady beat of his heart against my ear is comforting in a way I've never felt before. He smooths a hand through my hair and down my back before cupping my cheek.

His glowing green eyes meet mine, a strange mixture of pain and devotion behind them. "I vow to you that I will die before I allow anyone to ever harm you again, Elena."

"Who was that woman I saw in your mind?" I ask.

Even now, I can still feel the pain he felt when her image appeared, and I realize he is just as broken as I am.

His eyes are bright with unshed tears. "Someone I could not save."

He doesn't offer anything else, and I don't press him either. Instead, I wrap my arms around him.

If we are broken, we can be broken together.

Cold wind blows through the cavern, and he tucks the blanket tight around my shoulders as he holds me close.

"Rest now, Elena. I will keep watch."

Closing my eyes, I allow myself to fall away.

CHAPTER 24

VANEK

When morning comes, I observe as Elena sleeps trustingly in my arms. Inwardly, I curse myself for accidentally linking my mind to hers. I am glad she only saw a glimpse of Al'ora. Elena has enough nightmares of her own without me adding to them with mine.

Anger fills me as I think of everything she went through. I will die before I ever allow anyone to harm her again.

My nostrils flare as I detect someone nearby. Three distinct scents. I am not sure if they are Hunters or contestants. Either way, I do not wish to wait around to find out.

I gently shake Elena's shoulder to wake her. Her eyes snap open and widen immediately. "What's wrong?"

"I scent others nearby. We need to leave. Now."

All the color drains from her face. "If you can smell them, can't they tell we're here as well?"

I shake my head. "My people's sense of smell is more

acute than most other species, except for Lycaons and A'kai. We must move quickly and quietly."

She nods, and we begin packing our belongings. I loop the two packs to my front and kneel so she can climb onto my back.

Without hesitation, I climb up the rock wall of the waterfall. The scent of her fear permeates the air around us.

"Hold tightly to me."

I dig my claws into the rocky surface to gain purchase as I climb up toward the top of the falls. When I reach the edge, I pull us both over and scan the forest.

I do not detect anyone nearby, and a small sigh of relief escapes me.

The scent of the others is gone, telling me they are far enough away to not be a problem right now.

Elena looks at the surrounding forest. The trees are so tall they obscure our view of anything beyond the forest. We have to make it to the ice and snow part of the arena so we can locate the mountain as the Patikos instructed. But I can see nothing from down here to tell me where it is.

"Which way should we go?" she asks.

I lift my gaze to the thick tree canopy overhead. "I'll have to climb to see which direction we must go in. Wait here."

CHAPTER 25

ELENA

I watch as Vanek begins to climb up one of the nearby trees. The trunk so large it reminds me of the ancient sequoias of Terra. I know he just climbed up a rock wall, but I'm terrified he could fall.

As he disappears through the dense branches, I place my back to the tree and stare out at the woods, praying that nobody finds us here.

Several pieces of bark and orange, pine-like needles rain down onto the ground around me. I lift my head to find Vanek already crawling back down.

He releases his grip on the tree and jumps the last ten meters to the ground, stopping my heart. I rush over to him. "What were you thinking, letting yourself fall all that way?"

"That was nothing. A simple small leap."

"A small leap?" I ask incredulously. He could have broken his legs.

His brow furrows. "I do not understand. Why are you upset? I have found where we need to go."

I cross my arms over my chest. "I'm upset because you need to be careful. You could have been hurt."

"But I was not," he counters.

"Just... be careful next time. I don't want to lose you."

His expression softens.

I'm still so keyed up from having to run from the cave so quickly, my emotions are all over the place. Unable to help myself, I wrap my arms around him. "Promise me you won't leave me here alone?"

He returns my embrace and whispers in my hair. "I will not leave you, Elena."

I lift my face to his. The warmth of his breath fans across my skin. My gaze drops to his lips, and I am already imagining the taste of his kiss.

His glowing green eyes search mine as I slowly lean in. "Vanek, I—"

A sharp howl echoes through the forest, startling us both.

He clenches his jaw. "The Lycaon is in these woods."

I'm about to suggest we should search for him, but Vanek points up the river. "We must follow this until we reach another waterfall upstream. Then we must go left and cut across the desert."

"Desert?"

He nods. "It is part of the arena."

As much as this forest feels dark and foreboding, I'm dreading going through a desert. I hate the heat, and the idea of little water is terrifying. "How long do you think it will take to cross through the desert to the ice world part of the arena?"

He pauses a moment before answering. "It depends upon what we find there."

"What do you mean?"

"I assume this place is meant to have challenges for us:

predators and such that we must face in addition to the Hunters."

I swallow thickly. I hadn't even considered that. I was just worried about the other people in the arena with us and not about animals.

I palm the blaster rifle hanging off my shoulder. "At least we have these that we took from the Hunters."

He nods. "They do offer a decided advantage."

As we make our way along the river, I notice several tiny yellow flowers in the grass among the trees. As a botanist, I marvel at their ability to thrive with such little sun, given the dense forest canopy overhead. Then again, this is an alien world, and I can't expect everything to be like it is on Terra.

I make a mental note of each plant and tree we pass, thinking about my life as it once was. "You know, if this were any other situation, I could just imagine myself lost in here for days, studying all the new plants. That used to be my dream—xenobotany."

He turns to me. "When you are free of this place, you can pursue that dream."

"How?"

"Your people are just beginning to launch deep space ships of exploration."

I blink several times. "Why are they doing that? That's dangerous. They have no idea what's out here."

He nods. "My people agree. We have tried to dissuade them, but they do not wish to heed our warnings."

Tears sting my eyes as I think back on how naïve I was about space travel. I swallow against the lump in my throat. "If I had known then what I know now..." My voice trails off as dark memories fill my mind. "I was so foolish, Vanek." My voice quavers. "I thought going into space was an adventure. When I first got to Mars, I was so in awe of it, you know. It was this blank canvas in a way. A challenge to see what I could get to grow there. I just never considered the dangers, you know."

"You cannot blame yourself for what happened, Elena. You had no way of knowing what was out there." He pauses. "I was the same as you when I first joined the V'loryn Defense Force."

My eyes snap up to him.

He continues. "My people have been traveling the stars for thousands of years. And even though I was aware of the dangers, I did not think anything would happen to me. But I was wrong."

Sadness flits briefly across his normally impassive face. I take his hand. "What happened to you?"

He stares at the forest with a faraway look. "Forgive me," he murmurs. "But I cannot speak of it. Even now it is too… painful."

Despite his stoic expression, it is easy to read the pain behind his eyes. I loop my arm through his, wanting to offer him comfort.

Silence settles in the space between us as we walk side by side along the river.

I wish he trusted me with his pain. I know how lonely it is to carry something that devastating alone. But I also don't want to push him to speak about something he cannot.

As we continue, Vanek stops periodically to listen to the forest and scent the wind, checking to see if we are being tracked.

Movement in the bushes startles us, and he immediately pulls me behind him, standing protectively in front of me with his fangs bared and his claws fully extended.

Two lavender eyes peek out from between the leaves and something that looks like a cross between a dog and a lizard steps out of the foliage and cautiously approaches us.

With cute, pointed ears and a long tail with spikes down

the length, I watch as it begins to wag its tail and its tongue lolls out of its mouth. It's so cute, I'm surprised when Vanek doesn't instantly relax.

"Awww, look at him. He's precious."

I start to walk around Vanek, but he stops me short. "Elena, do not move."

Something about his tone sends fear skittering up my spine. "What is it?"

"Climb onto my back. Now."

"Wha—"

"Now," he insists.

Panic floods my system as I clamber onto his back. He turns and races through the woods with lightning speed. The forest and the trees blurring around me so quickly, I have to squeeze my eyes shut so I don't get dizzy.

A blast of light arcs past us, exploding on a nearby tree. It's followed quickly by another.

Without warning, Vanek leaps up into a tree and begins climbing so fast and so high, my heart pounds as I look down as the ground falls away beneath us, struggling not to scream.

He rushes out onto a branch and as it begins to bow under our combined weight, he jumps to another tree. He does this several times until I finally duck my head against his back, too scared to look down for fear that I'll lose my grip and tumble to my death.

After what feels like an eternity, we finally stop. My limbs tremble from holding on to him so tightly, that when he tells me it's safe to let go, I cannot make them respond.

Carefully, Vanek pulls me around to his front and drops his forehead gently to mine. "Elena, look at me," he whispers.

Reluctantly, I open my eyes. As soon as I see the branches all around us, panic tightens my chest. "We're still up in the trees?"

"Yes."

I draw in a shaking breath. "Those were Hunters, weren't they? How did they find us?"

He clenches his jaw. "They are using *dovars."*

"What are those?"

"That creature we saw in the woods," he explains. "Hunters use them to track prey."

"How did you not smell them?"

"They must have been using something to mask their scent from me," he says. "That is the only explanation that would make sense."

As his words sink in, fear twists deep inside me. Even with Vanek's superior senses, we're still not safe. Especially if the Hunters were able to get that close to us without him knowing.

He must read the concern in my expression, because he places two fingers up under my chin, tipping my face up to meet his. He darts a glance off to the left and the thick trunk of the tree. "You see how large this branch is?"

I nod. "We're going to stay up here for the night."

I swallow against the knot of worry in my stomach. "But… it's so far up. If we fall, we're dead."

He shakes his head. "I will not let you fall, Elena. My vow."

"Can't we find another cave or—"

"It is safest to remain up here. There is little chance Hunters would locate us quickly this high up or that they would be able to surprise us."

As I consider his explanation, it occurs to me that my legs are still wrapped around his waist and my arms around his neck. My heart pounds as I look down at the wide branch we're perched on. I tell myself that I need to let go of him, but I can't.

I'm too afraid to fall.

"Vanek?"

"Yes?"

"I need to tell you something and I want you to promise not to laugh."

He gives me a solemn nod. "My vow."

A nervous chuckle escapes me. "I know I was in the Terran Space program and that required flight and all, but... I'm actually kind of terrified of heights."

He blinks several times.

"I know. I know," I tell him. "It sounds really stupid when you think of what I did for a living, but there it is. The cold, hard truth."

He cocks his head to the side. "How is it that the idea of falling terrifies you more than the *dovar*?"

I shrug. "It was kind of cute, don't you think?"

He arches a brow. "No, I do not. It seems your species does not possess much of a self-preservation instinct."

My jaw drops, completely offended. I'm about to snap at him, but stop when I notice the slight quirk of his lips.

"You're teasing me, aren't you?"

He dips his chin as amusement dances behind his eyes.

Playfully, I hit at his shoulder. "Just promise not to let go of me all night and I'll stay up here as long as you want."

His gaze holds mine intensely. "Easily done."

CHAPTER 26

VANEK

She trusts me to not let her fall, despite her fears, and I cannot deny that it pleases me immensely to know this.

Even after I set her feet on the branch, she holds tightly to me with both arms, and I enjoy the contact between us.

I've observed my friend Marek and his bondmate Elizabeth enough that I always found it strange how tactile Terrans are compared to V'loryns. I'd often wondered if the physical touch and contact even bothered Marek, since it is not something frequently done, even among bondmates of my species.

But as Elena holds tightly to me, I find that I relish the feel of her arms wrapped around my form.

After I set up a tarp to shield us from any wind or rain, I sit down on the branch, leaning my back against the trunk as she sits across my lap and nestles against my chest as I hold her.

I have never known contentment like this.

If she would let me, I would hold her forever, if I could.

She lifts her gaze to me. "Are you sure this isn't uncomfortable for you?"

If she only knew how much I enjoyed holding her, she would never ask this. "Not at all. Your weight is very slight. It is not a burden to hold you like this."

She rests her head against my chest. "Thank you, Vanek."

"Of course."

After we eat some of the rations in our packs and drink some water, I tell her to sleep while I keep watch.

She shakes her head. "There's no way I'll be able to rest. Not up here."

This worries me. "Your people need far more rest than mine. You must sleep, Elena. We have a long journey still ahead of us."

She laughs softly. "Why are you always telling me to sleep? Is it because I talk too much?"

I enjoy the sound of her voice and could listen to her speak forever. "I assure that is not the case. I only insist upon you resting because your kind require far more sleep than mine."

I know. I just… I'm afraid I'll accidentally roll off your lap and fall if I go to sleep."

"I would never let that happen," I vow.

Her entire form is still tense against me. So I decide to try to distract her with conversation. "Did you have any companion animals when you were growing up?" I ask.

She nods. "I had a cat named Liam." A wistful smile crests her lips. "I found him when I was a little girl and he was just a kitten. I took him with me to college." She pauses. "He hated my boyfriend, Matt, so much that anytime Matt came over, Liam would scratch or bite at him."

Irrational jealousy fills me as she speaks of a former suitor at the same time that I find myself immeasurably grateful for her guardian feline keeping this male away from her.

She continues. “I suppose that should have been a sign for me that Matt was no good, but I ignored it at the time.”

I frown. “Why was he ‘no good?’ ”

“He kept trying to pressure me to sleep with him, but I wanted to wait. So… he ended up cheating on me, and it was devastating.”

“Matt was a fool to do this to you. I do not understand this behavior in Terran males.” I study her face, unable to fathom how any male could ever do something like this to her. “I have heard they often find it difficult to commit to one partner.”

“V’loryn guys aren’t like that?” she asks.

“No, we are not. When we mate, it is for life.”

Her mouth drifts open, but she quickly snaps it shut. “You said your friend Marek was married to a Terran, right?”

I nod.

“Are there a lot of interspecies marriages between your people and mine?”

“No. They are the first.”

“Wow. If Terran women find out how committed you guys are, I’ll bet there will be a lot more of those marriages in the near future.”

“Why do you say this?” I ask.

“Because what woman wouldn’t want a man that is completely committed to her? A guy that will not cheat or leave her for someone else…” Her voice trails off a moment before she frowns. “Do V’loryns date?”

“No. We are usually betrothed to someone when we are young. The Elders make the pairing, and when we reach the Age of Joining, we form the S’acris.”

“What is that?”

“The S’acris is the permanent mental bond created

between mated pairs. It allows for the exchange of thought and emotion with our bondmate."

"Are you betrothed to someone, Vanek?"

I shake my head. "As I mentioned earlier, I have decided against taking a mate."

"Because of the Aerilon woman I saw in your mind?" she asks. "Is it because you loved her?"

In a way, I suppose I did. "It is not as you think, Elena. It is… more complicated than that."

CHAPTER 27

ELENA

The pain in his eyes makes my heart clench. Without thinking, I take Vanek's hand, wanting only to offer him comfort.

The moment my bare skin touches his, images and emotions crash through my mind like waves upon the shore of my consciousness.

The image of the Aerilon woman appears before me and pain so great I can barely contain it fills me until I feel as if I'm drowning in it, and I realize it is not my pain… it is his.

"You should not be here, Elena," his mind speaks to mine.

Vanek pulls me back from the connection. My eyes blink several times as they readjust to our surroundings. "What was—"

"Forgive me," he whispers, sorrow breaking through his normally passive expression. "I did not have my mental transference shields up. I did not mean to pull you into the al'nara again."

"It's all right," I reply. "It's not your fault. It's mine. I shouldn't have touched you."

He clenches his jaw. "I should have had more control."

"Vanek, you don't have to apologize."

He gives me a sorrowful look. "You do not understand, Elena. I do not want to risk you experiencing… what happened. It is too terrible and I—"

"It's all right," I whisper softly. "I'm fine."

He studies me a moment and it is easy to read the guilt behind his eyes. "I should be more careful with you." He drops his forehead gently to mine. "You are the last person I ever want to cause any pain."

"You haven't, Vanek. You've taken care of me. You've protected me." I cup his cheek. "I would probably be dead already if not for you."

His eyes shine with sadness and I hate that he feels bad. I'm fine, but he doesn't want to believe it. So, instead, I decide to change the subject. "Tell me more about your sister."

He sighs. "L'Tana is a Healer. So naturally, she believes she knows everything. Even when she does not."

I laugh. "My sister is the same way. She thinks everyone else is wrong, except for her."

A hint of a smile quirks his lips.

"Does she live close to you?"

He nods. "We both live on the estate with my father." He shakes his head softly. "Only a few weeks ago, she brought a Terran male over for evening meal with us."

"Uh oh," I tease. "That sounds pretty serious."

"That is what I am concerned about." He purses his lips. "Although she will not admit it to me, I suspect she is already in love with him. They work together at the embassy. He is a Terran doctor."

"Well, maybe he's a good guy," I offer. "I mean… is your

sister old enough for this 'Age of Joining' that you were talking about?"

His cheeks and the tips of his ears turn light green in what I imagine must be his version of a blush. "Yes, but... it is only the males of my kind that experience this."

"What do you mean?"

"The Age of Joining happens between twenty-eight and thirty-three cycles, when a male experiences his first mating cycle."

I frown. "Mating cycle?"

He swallows hard and then nods. "It is... a mating heat of sorts, and it lasts for three to five days."

CHAPTER 28

VANEK

Her jaw drops, but she quickly snaps it shut. "That sounds... intense," she offers.

"I have heard that it can be."

Even as I explain this, I am acutely aware of everything about her. As my Si'an T'kara, my body, it seems, is already completely attuned to her own. I am twenty-nine cycles old, and I am concerned that if I remain in her proximity when she reaches the fertile peak of her monthly cycle, it may trigger my mating heat.

I do not share this with her, however. If my mating cycle approaches, I will have to do my best to ignore and suffer through it somehow.

As I think about this, the more pressing matter of my withdrawal comes to the forefront of my mind. The slight tremor in my hands indicates that I need another half pill, but I am loath to take it, knowing that the last pulled me under and into a sleep so deep I was unable to prevent myself from linking with Elena's mind.

Even now, my withdrawals are the reason it is so difficult to maintain my mental transference shields.

I glance down at the wound on her arm from where we removed the tracker. It is closed, and scabbed over, but it is yet another reminder of my failings. If not for my addiction, I could use the Balance to heal her completely.

My kind are able to take from nature to heal our own wounds. But those who are blessed with the fated bond can heal their bondmates as well. My friend Marek did this with Elizabeth, saving her life when she would have died.

But it requires a great deal of energy, not just from nature, but also ourselves. We serve as conduits for the energy that would be used to heal our mates.

Because of my addiction, I doubt I'd have enough energy to do this for her. It can be dangerous as well to wield the Balance.

In my current state, I could die in the attempt, leaving her to face the Great Hunt alone.

When Marek used the Balance to save Elizabeth it nearly killed him. He was unconscious for several days after.

I am ashamed of myself. She deserves so much better than me. I should be able to use the Balance to heal a simple injury.

A low howl sounds in the distance, and she stills. "Is that the Lycaon—Ryker?"

I nod. Although I am hesitant to trust him, I am beginning to believe that I should, at least, approach him about his offer of a possible alliance between us. He claims his people treasure females and protect them, regardless of species.

It is a risk to trust him at his word, but I may soon have no choice. I have seen no sign of the Mosauran. If I go into full withdrawal, Elena will need someone else to watch over her while I am incapacitated.

He howls again, this time closer, and that makes the decision for me. "Elena, there is something I must tell you."

"What is it?"

But as she lifts her eyes to me, they are shining with such trust that it breaks my resolve. I know that the secret I carry will cause her distress and make her afraid, when the only thing I want to do is assuage all her fears and promise her that I will keep her safe.

Ryker's howls fill the air, and I wonder why he is so vocal. Does he not realize that his sounds could lead the Hunters to him?

A sudden realization hits me. He, alone, is the only one who knows my secret aside from the masters who put me in the arena. I believe he is trying to reach out to me, alerting me to his general location so I might seek him out.

He said that Lycaons treasure females. He knows if we stay in the arena too long, I will suffer withdrawal and put Elena in danger.

I clench my jaw as I study her face. I *have* to find the Lycaon. And when I do, I must find a way to make her go with him and leave me behind if I begin to falter. I will not be the reason she is caught. I refuse to put her in any more danger than she already is.

I decide against telling her about my addiction. There will be no need once I find the Lycaon. "I think we should seek out Ryker tomorrow," I tell her.

She blinks several times. "But, I thought—"

"You were right," I cut her off. "We need allies."

"What about the Mosauran? You said you have a treaty with their people."

"I do not know how to find him," I explain. "But the Lycaon—" I pause as he howls again. "I believe *he* is searching for *us*."

CHAPTER 29

ELENA

Sleeping in Vanek's arms makes me feel safe despite the danger I know we're in. His warm cinnamon scent surrounds me as I rest my head against his chest. He tightens his hold on me, shifting slightly as he wraps the blankets around us like a cocoon.

"Are you warm enough?" he whispers against the shell of my ear.

My heart flutters in my chest. "Yes."

My mind drifts to all the times I've dreamed of him over the past few years. This is exactly how we would sit together. He would hold me against him and I'd rest my head against his chest, below his chin.

My thoughts return to the image of the Aerilon woman in his mind, when we were linked in the al'nara, and I wonder again about their relationship. Was she a friend? A lover?

Whoever she was, he was attached to her. He said it was complicated. I could feel his intense sadness as he gazed at her, as if it were my own.

"You should rest, Elena. I will stay awake and keep guard."

"You need to sleep too."

He shakes his head. "I will not risk falling asleep and accidentally linking my mind with yours again." He pauses. "I will not put you through that."

"It's all right," I tell him. "It wasn't—" I stop abruptly, casting about for the right word before settling on, "bad, if that's what you're worried about."

"You do not understand," he murmurs. "In my culture, it is forbidden to even touch anyone who is not your bondmate or family. And linking with someone's mind in the al'nara is only done between bondmates."

"Why?"

"Because it is the most intimate connection one can ever experience with another. All of their hopes, thoughts, dreams… emotions, can all be shared within the al'nara." He sighs. "I am fortunate that I maintained enough control when we were linked that I was able to partition some of my mind from yours."

I still. "What could have happened if you hadn't? Does it hurt people that are not V'loryn?"

"If I hadn't, you would experience my pain as if it were your own. And I refuse to do that to you."

"My people may not link minds," I tell him. "But we do share each other's pain. We do it out of love. No one should have to suffer in silence, alone."

He studies me a moment, his green eyes searching mine. "And I would shield you from any and all harm if I could, including the pain that I carry."

I rest my head against his chest, listening to the steady beat of his heart beneath my ear.

He smooths a hand down my back. "I am broken, Elena. And I want only to spare you this pain."

Another howl sounds in the distance and Vanek sighs heavily, and the moment is gone.

He arches a brow. "It seems Ryker does not wish us to get any sleep."

I laugh softly at the irritation he tries, but fails to hide. "Perhaps not."

We talk for a while longer, until I can't keep my eyes open anymore. When I fall asleep, I know without doubt that Vanek will keep me safe.

CHAPTER 30

VANEK

In the morning, we pack up our supplies and move through the trees for a few hours before finally returning to the forest floor at Elena's insistence.

She says the heights make her too sick, and she begged for a reprieve.

As I gently set her feet on the ground, I arch a brow. "We will only travel down here for a short while so that you may recover from your nausea. But then, we must return to the trees. It is safer up there."

She nods.

"I can carry you if you'd like."

"I'm fine, Vanek. Really." She smiles warmly at me. "Besides, I should use my legs a bit while I can before you have to carry us through the trees again."

"You are no burden to carry," I reassure her.

She grins. "You're kind, Vanek, but it's not as if I weigh nothing either."

If she only knew how much the slight weight of her form

worries me. She is fragile, my mate. I understand now why my friend Marek is often concerned for his bondmate, Elizabeth.

Their bones are delicate compared to ours and their weight negligible. As much as I wish I could claim Elena as my bondmate, I am almost glad I cannot. I believe I would be too worried that I might accidentally hurt her upon our first mating.

Several flowers grow along the forest floor. I observe as their vibrant orange petals begin to slowly unfurl.

"Those are lovely," Elena says. "I've never seen blooms like this."

She leans down and plucks one. A faint dusting of pollen shakes loose, floating around us. She takes another and more pollen swirls on the wind.

"It smells lovely." She smiles.

She is right. It has a sweet scent. Not overpowering, but pleasant.

She tucks one of the flowers in her hair, and I am completely mesmerized as I stare down at her, transfixed by her beauty. Try as I might, I cannot stop staring.

In the back of my mind, it occurs to me that the pollen may be affecting me somehow, but I find I don't care. Not at this moment.

I reach out and gently tuck a stray tendril of hair behind her ear. "*You* are lovely," I murmur. "More beautiful than anything I have ever seen."

A stunning smile crests her lips, and as my gaze drops to her mouth, I find myself wondering if her lips are as soft as I've imagined.

Unable to stop myself, I curl my arms around her form and pull her to me as my *tr'llen* begins low in my chest.

"You purr?" She smiles.

I arch a brow. "It is not a purr. It is a tr'llen. It is meant to entice. We do this when we desire someone," the words escape my lips before I even realize I've said them aloud.

Her warm brown eyes search mine a moment before she stretches up on her toes until her face is nearly level with mine. "And do your people kiss?" she whispers.

I have seen Marek and Elizabeth kiss many times, but it is not something normally done among my kind. I shake my head. "V'loryns do not kiss."

She leans in and the warm mint of her breath fans across my skin a moment before she presses her lips softly to mine.

Her lips are warm and softer than I imagined. I open my mouth and her tongue finds my own, curling around it.

At first, our kiss is gentle and exploring, but it soon turns into something more urgent. I lift her into my arms as her mouth repeatedly meshes with mine until one kiss blurs into another and I'm not sure where one ends and another begins.

I am completely lost in sensation as I run my fingers through her hair and down her back. I back her against a nearby tree, and she wraps her legs around me.

She moans as I roll my hips against hers. I want her more than I have ever wanted anything before. I long to seal her to me and claim her as my mate.

"Vanek." She whispers my name, bringing me back into awareness.

I cannot claim her as mine. I cannot bind myself to her.

I pull back, and she stares up at me in confusion. "What's wrong?"

I shake my head. "I cannot do this."

"Why?"

A flash of light catches my eye. Panic stops my heart and I only have a moment to try to pull her away, but it is too late as the energy net throws up a wall between us, trapping her.

"Vanek!" She beats against the glowing barrier, her eyes wide with fear.

I do the same, clenching my teeth to suppress my roar of anger, desperate to free her.

Closing my eyes, I force myself to think rationally. It is difficult when every instinct inside me demands that I throw myself at the barrier until it breaks, even though I know that would not work.

I dart a glance at our surroundings before I find the small device that powers the net. It is near the edge of the trap by our feet.

I kneel, pointing it out to her. "I will have to disable it."

She studies the small box curiously. "Can you crush it? Make it stop working that way?"

I shake my head. "If I cannot disable it carefully, I could trigger a secondary mechanism that would kill us both."

"What?" Her eyes widen. "How?"

"By increasing the energy output of the net to deliver a shock that would stop both of our hearts."

She swallows hard. "Do you think you can disable it?"

I nod. "I have done it before, when I was on the Defense Force."

She smiles. "Good."

I turn my attention back to the box, but she stops me abruptly. "Vanek?"

"Yes?"

She places her palm against the barrier, and I do the same, desperately wishing I could touch her. Her gaze holds mine as she speaks softly. "Whatever happens… if you hear someone coming, I want you to leave me behind and save yourself."

I jerk my head back. "I will never leave you."

"You'd have to. I don't want you to get caught, Vanek. I—"

I meet her gaze evenly. "We live together or we die together. Do you understand? I will never leave you, Elena. Never!"

CHAPTER 31

ELENA

His words melt my heart. Vanek is a good man.

Reluctantly, I nod.

As he works, the sun makes its way across the sky until it begins a slow descent on the horizon, lengthening the shadows of the trees all around us.

I observe as he meticulously picks apart wires, tracing them to their origins and then shaking his head in frustration and starting again when he realizes he still has not found the correct one.

As I watch him work, it occurs to me that he might not be able to free me. This is obviously a Hunter's trap. If they were to come, Vanek would have to leave me here so he could escape. This might be the last time I ever see him.

The prospect of my demise makes me bold as I lean against the barrier and place my palm against it, wishing so much that I could touch him. "I dreamed of you, you know."

He stops and slowly lifts his head, a questioning look on his face. "What do you mean?"

"Before we met," I explain. "I used to dream of you."

Something—an emotion I cannot quite discern—flickers behind his eyes, but it is gone too quickly for me to know what it is. "Tell me of your dreams," he says softly.

"Your face was hidden in shadow, but I could always make out the tips of your ears." A wistful smile crests my lips as I study them. "You would come to me in my dreams when I was sad or scared and alone. I would sit with you, as we did in the tree. You would comfort me. You called me your Si'an T'kara," I whisper. "But you never told me what it means."

His mouth drifts open. "How do you know these words?"

"You said them to me in my dreams. It was your voice, Vanek. I recognized your voice the moment you saved me." A tear slips down my cheek. "I was so afraid it was a dream when you rescued me. That I would wake up and find myself all alone again. But when I woke up… you were there."

I place my palm on the glass. His gaze holds mine as he does the same. "What do those words mean? What is Si'an T'kara?"

His eyes are bright with unshed tears. "Fated One," he whispers. "The other half of my soul."

"Did you dream of me?" I ask softly. "Did you dream of me before we met?"

He shakes his head. "But I knew the moment your eyes met mine, when you woke up in the med bay. I knew then what you were to me." His glowing green eyes stare deep into mine with a strange mixture of love and pain reflecting behind them. "You are my Si'an T'kara—my Fated One."

"Why didn't you say anything?" I ask, even as I realize that I said nothing either.

"Because I cannot have you, Elena. No matter how much—"

A piercing howl echoes through the woods, and Vanek's head snaps toward the sound, scanning for Ryker. His claws lengthen, and he bares his fangs as he snarls. "I know you are near. Reveal yourself."

Glowing orange eyes stare back at us from the darkness as a dark brown wolf, larger than any I've ever seen on Terra, walks toward us.

Panic claws at my chest. "Vanek, run! You have to get out of here before—"

I stop short as the wolf transforms into a man. When he lifts his head, I recognize Ryker immediately. "How did you do that?"

He gives me a lopsided grin. "My kind are shifters. That was my *wolven* form, and this is my two-legged form."

As I stare at him, I realize he's completely nude. My gaze travels down his muscular form, and I notice only a long vertical line on his skin where normal male anatomy would be.

He arches a brow. "I'm sure I seem strange to you, but I assure you, I mean you no harm."

Vanek narrows his eyes. "You've been tracking us."

Although he says this as a statement, Ryker obviously recognizes it's a question as well. "Yes." He looks at the box in Vanek's hand. "And it looks as though you need help."

Vanek arches a brow. "You know how to disarm this?"

"Yes," Ryker replies firmly. "Hunters use those to try to trap my kind illegally on my home world."

My mouth drifts open as I think about how horrible that must be for them.

"Stand aside. I will disarm it quickly"

As he approaches, Vanek growls low in his chest.

Ryker meets his eyes evenly. "I promise you that I can free your mate. Please, just let me try."

Vanek looks to me, and I nod. He places his palm to the barrier again, and I do the same. "It will be all right," I whisper.

His glowing green eyes search mine before he gives me a subtle nod.

He steps back, and Ryker picks up the box and begins tracing the wires with one long, sharp claw as I hold my breath, praying that he doesn't shock and kill us both.

CHAPTER 32

VANEK

As Ryker works, panic claws at my throat. The acrid scent of Elena's fear fills the air, calling my primal instincts to protect and defend my mate. A low growl rumbles in my chest as I glare at Ryker.

Without bothering to look away from his task, he addresses me. "You getting angry at me is not going to make this go any faster, you know."

Instantly, I stop and go still. A slight tremor begins in my hands, and I am uncertain if it is worry or withdrawal that causes this. I only know that I am desperate for him to free Elena.

A quick flash of light and the energy barrier disappears.

Unable to stop myself, I rush toward Elena. I pull her into my arms, holding her close to my chest.

Still holding her against me, I lift my gaze to Ryker and dip my chin. "Thank you."

He narrows his eyes. "I did it for her. Not you, V'loryn."

The sound of voices carries on the wind, and my head

snaps toward the forest. "Hunters," I say under my breath. "We have to go."

Ryker gestures off to the left. "You go in that direction. I'll go the opposite and lead them away."

His offer stuns me. "Why do you help us?"

"I already told you. I do it for her, but—"

"But what?" I snap, wanting to understand his motivations. Is he the ally Elena believes he could be to us? Or will he try to take her from me the first chance he gets?

Even the mere thought of him trying to take her fills me with fierce possessiveness. I gather her in my arms, holding her close to my chest as I glare at him. "Tell me," I demand. "Are you friend? Or are you foe?"

"If I was your enemy, you would not still be standing here unscathed, V'loryn." His head whips back toward the forest in the direction of the voices. "Now, go. Before it is too late."

Without hesitation, I position Elena on my back and race away through the forest and toward the desert quadrant. Night is almost upon us, and I must find shelter before then. I do not want to be without cover in the dark. Especially when I am unsure of what nocturnal creatures may hunt this area.

CHAPTER 33

ELENA

I hold tightly to Vanek as we race through the woods, praying the Hunters are not following us. I think of Ryker, hoping that he's all right. I know Vanek doesn't entirely trust him, but he helped us when he didn't have to. It would have been easier for him to continue on his way and just leave us there in the trap. That he didn't do this, speaks volumes about his character.

"Do you think Ryker will be all right?" I ask.

A low growl rumbles Vanek's chest before he responds. "He is a Lycaon. He will be fine."

"Why do you dislike him so much?"

Instead of answering, he slows a bit as we approach another river. Worry fills me when I notice how wide it is and how fast the current flows. "We will have to cross, but we must find a safe location to do so," he says, and I realize he hasn't answered my question.

As we move along the riverbank, I ask it again. "Why do you dislike Ryker so much? Even after he helped us?"

Vanek kneels down far enough for me to easily climb off his back. He turns to me. His gaze holds mine with a look somewhere between guilt and possession. "You are right. He helped us. But I… I believe the fated bond is affecting me."

"What do you mean?"

"I feel possessive of you… aggressive toward anyone who would dare even come near you." He sighs. "I have tried to fight it, but it is… a compulsion of my biology. A possessive instinct."

"So, why did you push me away when we kissed?"

His eyes snap to mine. "Forgive me. I should not have kissed you, Elena. It was wrong."

"Why was it wrong?"

"Because I cannot take you as mine."

"Is it because of her? The Aerilon woman I saw in the mind link?"

Sadness flits briefly across his expression before he nods. My heart sinks. "Do you still love her?"

"It is… more complicated than that."

"How?"

He clenches his jaw. "I cannot speak of it. Please, do not ask me to."

Swallowing hard, I nod even though I want to demand that he tell me.

"We must concentrate on finding a way across," he says, changing the subject. "Until we do, we are not safe."

We walk along the riverbank in awkward silence. I want to talk to him, but I'm not even sure where to begin. We barely know each other and yet, I've dreamed of him for so long, I feel as if I've known him forever… that I've waited for him for so many years, only to find that he doesn't want me.

I am simply a burden to him. Nothing more.

CHAPTER 34

VANEK

As I search for a way to cross, I clench my jaw at the slight tremor in my hands. It is my withdrawal coming on. I should take another half pill, but I dare not do it while we are traveling. I cannot afford to have my senses dulled while we are searching for a place to shelter.

But I cannot afford to be incapacitated either. I look at Elena, and a deep ache settles in my chest. I am a danger to her. I should have insisted that Ryker come with us. He helped us, proving that he is not a threat or danger to us. Elena will need an ally if something happens to me.

Curling my hands into fists, I struggle to still their trembling.

Elena walks up beside me. Her delicate scent carries on the wind, completely surrounding me with her intoxicating scent. Everything inside me wants to claim her.

It is taking every bit of my control to keep my distance.

When we kissed, I could think of nothing but joining my body and mind to hers, sinking my teeth deep into her neck and claiming her as my mate.

My withdrawals are eroding my controls, and I worry that I will be tempted to claim her if we are not rescued soon.

My mind snaps back to the present when I notice a series of flat stones that span the river. Close enough together that we should be able to traverse the water and reach the other side. It is odd that they are so evenly spaced, but I know this is an arena set up for the Great Hunt. Perhaps this was made this way.

My eyes scan the opposite bank, searching for any sign of a trap, but I see none.

A bright light above us catches my eye. When I look up, I notice a hovering vidcam, no doubt sending video of us toward the sick people that watch this event.

I grind my teeth. All the more reason for us to find shelter where we cannot be watched.

Elena notices it too. "What's that?"

"A vidcam. It is filming us."

She glares up at it. "The people who watch these things are disgusting."

"I agree."

I gesture to the stones. "I've found a way for us to cross."

Elena looks at the stones. "Those are spaces equidistant apart. Why do you think that is?"

A smile quirks my lips. She is observant and wise.

"I believe they may have been placed there intentionally."

"Do you think it's safe to cross then?"

"I do not know, but we have to try. This is the way toward the ice world part of the arena."

She nods.

I turn to her. "Let me carry you across."

"I should be able to—"

"If it is a trap, I am able to jump farther and run faster than you, Elena."

Reluctantly, she agrees. "All right. Let's go."

CHAPTER 35

VANEK

I gather Elena in my arms and then step onto the first stone. It is easy to reach the next and the one beyond that, but still, I go slow, worried that if I were to rush, I might lose my footing and fall into the swift current.

I'm not sure how deep it is, but I do not want to find out.

I'm only halfway across when I feel a sudden shift beneath my feet. I look down and notice the rocks are sinking, being swallowed up by the turbulent water.

Panic tightens my chest. This was a trap, just as I'd feared.

"Vanek?" Elena's worried voice calls out. "What's happening?"

"We're sinking. Hold on."

As the rocks begin to descend beneath the water, I rush over them, desperate to maintain my footing as I make my way across the river, knowing that if I fail, we could drown.

The acrid scent of Elena's fear floods my nostrils as I race to cross before we're swept away.

It's difficult to keep my footing now that the stones are

fully submerged. The swift current pulls at my feet and ankles, trying to rip us away and into the turbulent waters.

I take another step, my boot slips, and the world shifts into slow motion as we plunge into the icy water below.

Panic rips through me, and a muffled cry escapes my throat as I sink to the bottom of the river. I use all of my strength to push Elena toward the shore, satisfied when I see her feet touch the riverbed as she finds her footing.

Forcing myself to remain conscious, I move my arms and kick my legs fiercely, attempting to push up from the riverbed. But it is no use. My dense body weight makes swimming nearly impossible, and I sink again once more.

Detecting a muffled voice from above, I notice Elena standing on the banks of the river through the wavering haze of the water, but I cannot understand what she is saying.

Desperate for air, my lungs burn. The desire to inhale threatening to overwhelm me. As my oxygen begins to deplete, my emotions break to the surface.

I think of Elena and the way her lips felt against mine. The way her warm brown eyes stared deep into my own when I told her that she was my Fated One—my Si'an T'kara.

She is mine. How could I ever have thought I could deny this? How could I ever think that I would be able to push her away when everything within me wants only to pull her even closer, wrap my arms around her and never let her go.

A muffled splash draws my attention, and I look up to see Elena swimming toward me. Dressed in only her undergarments, I notice she is holding on to the sleeve of her clothing, and it is tied to one of the emergency blankets.

She cups my face, forcing my gaze to hers as her warm brown eyes search mine.

Through the touch of her skin against my own, I open a connection between us. *"Elena,"* I whisper in her thoughts. *"Save yourself. You must leave me."*

"No!" The word arcs through me with such conviction that it stills my heart.

"Eh'leh-na." I whisper the words for *I love you* in the ancient V'loryn tongue as she leans in and seals her mouth over mine, breathing air into my burning lungs.

My heart rate slows and when she pulls back, she wraps her arms around me, tying the cloth around my waist. She takes my hand and then places it on the material. *"Pull,"* her mind speaks to mine. *"Hurry."*

Hand over hand, I begin to drag myself along the river bottom and up the slope to the shore. She pulls with me.

When we finally break the surface, both of us are gasping for air. Panting heavily, we fall over onto the muddy shoreline on our back, staring up at the sky.

I glance over at her and find my strength renewed before I notice her shivering. I quickly stand and pull her up with me. I notice the blanket and her clothes still fastened around a nearby boulder and untie them.

She is shivering, so I quickly help her redress. The material of her suit is already dry and will help to warm her. I scan the surrounding area and start toward a cliff wall up ahead. Several dark spots on the rock face tell me it is full of caverns. Surely, one of them will be suitable enough to shelter in for the evening.

I lift her into my arms and cup her chin, tipping her face up to mine. "Hold on to me. I am going to have to climb. Do you think you can manage?"

Weakly, she nods.

CHAPTER 36

ELENA

Vanek's claws lengthen, and he uses them to stab at the earth and rock as he scales the cliff face wall. I hold tightly to him. With my arms and legs wrapped around his front, his powerful form moves beneath me. Thick layers of muscle rippling with every movement he makes.

I bury my face against his chest and breathe deep of his masculine scent to calm my nerves as he continues to climb high above the ground.

After what feels like forever, he grabs on to a ledge and pulls us inside a large cavern.

Quickly, he opens our packs and pulls out the second blanket, wrapping it tightly around me.

He hands me food and water. "Eat and drink this. You need this for your strength."

I'm still shaking a bit, so I don't bother to answer or argue.

I watch as he lays the other blanket out on a nearby rock

to dry. When he is finished, he turns back to me. He crosses the cavern and positions himself behind me, settling me across his lap as he wraps his strong arms around me.

I turn back to him, a question burning in the back of my mind. "When we were underwater… those words you spoke to me in your tongue… what do they mean?"

"Eh'leh-na," he whispers as his gaze holds mine intensely. "They are the ancient V'loryn words for I love you."

I still even as hope blooms in my chest. "But I thought—" I start but stop. "You pushed me away, and I thought you didn't want me. That I had done something wrong."

His glowing green eyes meet mine. "I long more than anything to take you as my bondmate," he whispers. "I have never loved anyone as I love you now."

Tears sting my eyes, but I blink them back.

"You are my Si'an T'kara, and I could have died, and you never would have known how I feel."

"How do you feel?"

His eyes travel over me, as if memorizing the contours of my face. He takes my hand and places it on his chest, directly over his heart. "I have pushed you away when everything inside me only wants to pull you closer. I long more than anything to make you mine, Elena. But I am afraid."

"Of what?"

"The things I have seen… the trauma I carry inside… I cannot let it touch you. I do not want you to experience the nightmares and the horrors. I—"

I press my finger to his lips to silence him. "You are not the only one with nightmares. We have both been through things that no one else should ever have to endure." I press my lips gently to his. "Share your pain with me. Let me be the one to help you."

"I am broken, Elena."

I cup his cheek. "We can be broken together, Vanek. And

together we can find a way to heal. I love you." A smile crests my lips. "I loved you even in my dreams... before I ever knew you were real."

He crushes his mouth to mine in a searing kiss, stealing the breath from my lungs.

I shift above him and turn to face him, straddling his thighs with my hips as he holds me tight to his chest. So close, I can feel his heart beating against mine.

He runs his fingers through my hair, gripping the long strands and tipping my head back as he kisses a trail of fire down my neck.

The tips of his fangs graze my already sensitive flesh as he traces his tongue along the pulsing artery of my neck.

I tip my head to the side, offering him better access, but he pulls back.

His eyes swirl from glowing green to obsidian black as he stares back at me, his fangs fully extended. If he were anyone else, I would be afraid, but it's Vanek, and I'm not.

"You do not fear me?" he whispers.

"Never." Cupping the back of his neck, I pull his lips back to mine. He opens his mouth and my tongue curls around his, deepening our kiss.

I'm breathless as he devours me with his lips and his tongue, branding me with the intense heat of his kiss.

I undo the fasteners on his tunic and slide it back and off his shoulders. I trace the tips of my fingers along the hard planes of muscle that line his abdomen and chest. The thick cords along his arms flex and ripple beneath my touch as he removes my clothing as well, until I'm only wearing my undergarments.

His length is a hard bar between us, and I gasp when I realize that only a thin scrap of fabric separates him from my entrance.

He groans as I roll my hips against his. "My l'ok is very

sensitive," he rasps. "If we do not stop now, I will be tempted to claim you."

"What if I want to be claimed?" I ask.

He growls low in arousal and then reaches a hand between us. He pulls aside the triangular scrap of fabric that separates us, and I gasp as he drags his fingers through my already slick folds.

His gaze holds mine, full of fire and possession. "Your scent is intoxicating," he rasps.

When he reaches the small bundle of nerves at the apex, a soft moan escapes my lips.

As he concentrates his attention on that sensitive pearl of flesh, I arch into him, wanting more.

I've touched myself before, but it has never felt anything like this.

His touch is fire, and I am completely lost in sensation. I moan out his name as he slips one finger inside me and then brushes his thumb over the small bundle of nerves that sends my desire even higher.

My entire body goes taut like a bowstring, and then I'm coming harder than I ever have before as wave after wave of pleasure moves over and through me.

He kisses me long and deep, stealing the breath from my lungs.

"Vanek," I barely manage. "That was… there are no words."

His gaze holds mine as he carefully lays me back on the stone floor and rolls me beneath him. He reaches down and touches my face, studying me with a look of intense love and devotion. "May I taste you," he whispers.

Warmth fills me as desire pulses through my veins. Unable to speak through my desire, I nod.

He leans down and captures my mouth in a claiming kiss until I'm breathless and panting beneath him.

He pulls down my bra, freeing my breasts.

The soft scrape of his teeth against the sensitive peak of my left breast makes me arch up against him. I run my fingers through his hair as he begins a gentle suction that drives me mad.

"Vanek." His name escapes my lips on a soft moan as he turns his attention to my other breast before moving down my body to my center.

Carefully, he parts my thighs, baring me to his gaze. His eyes are full of desire as they meet mine. "You are perfect," he whispers.

He dips his head between my thighs, and I gasp when he drags his tongue through my folds. He concentrates his attention on the softly hooded flesh at the apex as I dig my heels into his shoulders.

He growls, and the vibration moves straight through me. I arch up against him, biting my bottom lip to stifle the cry of pleasure that escapes me.

"Vanek, please," I whisper, and I don't even know what I'm asking for.

He brushes his tongue over the small pearl of flesh between my thighs and then begins a gentle suction. My every muscle goes tense a moment before stars explode behind my eyes as my orgasm sweeps over and through me, this time more intense than the last.

He presses a tender kiss to my inner thigh and then moves back up my body, sealing his mouth over mine in a branding kiss.

I reach for his l'ok, and he growls as I allow my fingers to trace over the ridges along his length. Heat pools deep in my core as I imagine what he might feel like inside me. He's so big, I cannot quite reach my fingers all the way around his length.

He growls as I swipe my thumb over the tip of his l'ok

and then wraps his hand around my wrist, pulling my hand away.

I stare up at him in confusion.

He cups my cheek. "I will not claim you here."

"Why not?"

"When I claim you, I will take you many times on the night of our first joining."

My entire body flushes with warmth. I cup the back of his neck and pull his lips down to mine, kissing him long and deep. When he pulls back, he pulls me with him as he lies on his side, holding me tight to his chest.

I'm not sure how long we lie there as I drift in and out of sleep, resting peacefully beside him, before he gently brushes the hair back from my face and then presses a tender kiss to my lips. "We should dress in case we must leave quickly."

After we both change back into our clothes, he wraps me in his arms and tugs the blanket around us, cocooning me in his warmth and his masculine scent. Closing my eyes, I allow myself to fall away as he whispers words of devotion in the ancient V'loryn tongue.

CHAPTER 37

VANEK

As Elena falls asleep in my arms, the tremors of my hands grow stronger. I reach into my pocket, meaning to take only a quarter of one neural relaxer, not wanting to risk falling into a deep sleep where I cannot wake quickly or where I might accidentally link my mind to hers in the al'nara.

I still and panic stops my heart when I feel nothing but soft mush in my pocket. I pull my hand away and see the remnants of the pills, coating my fingers. They must have started to dissolve when we fell in the water.

Desperate, I bring my fingers to my lips. The moment the paste dissolves under my tongue, I wait anxiously for the sweeping relief through my body, praying the shaking will stop immediately, but it does not.

Whatever properties they contained that made them effective have been lost.

As I gaze down at Elena, lying so trustingly in my embrace, I know that I must tell her the truth. I have to.

And with this revelation comes another: I have to find Ryker. Even though all my possessive instincts demand that I keep him away from my mate, I need him to help me protect her.

I will go into full withdrawal without my pills, and she will be alone and without help. It would leave her vulnerable, and I could not live with myself if anything happened to her because of my inability to be there for her.

As if my very thoughts have summoned him, I hear a low howl in the distance and know that Ryker is near.

Carefully, I untangle myself from Elena's arms and quietly move to the front of the cavern. I scan the forest below us and a pair of glowing orange eyes blinks up at me from the darkness.

I gesture for him to come up and then watch as he scales the cliff face wall. As soon as he reaches the ledge, I signal him to be quiet since Elena is still asleep.

Ryker moves to my side. His gaze darts to Elena before returning to mine.

"How are you doing?" His eyes drop to my trembling hands, and I know he is asking about my withdrawal symptoms.

"I am fine. For now." The lie brands my tongue.

He arches a brow, unconvinced, and I realize I cannot withhold the truth from him.

"I do not have any neural relaxers left. It is only a matter of time before I go into withdrawal."

"Does she know?"

I shake my head. "I did not wish to distress her. Besides, if we are rescued soon, there may be no reason to tell her."

He frowns. "Your people form permanent mental bonds when they mate. How are you concealing this from her?"

"She is not—" I start, but stop abruptly. "I have not bonded with her."

His nostrils flare. "The smell of this cavern suggests otherwise. She reeks of your scent and you hers. Why would you dishonor her by taking her to your bed but not binding her to you? I know your kind do not take mates outside of your race. Is it because she is not V'loryn?"

"Tread carefully, Lycaon." I growl low in my throat. "You know not of what you speak. I would never dishonor my Si'an T'kara."

"And yet you withhold the truth from her about your condition."

I clench my jaw. He is right. I should have told her the truth before now. I glance down at my trembling hands. "She will know soon enough," I reply darkly.

He opens his mouth to speak, but I cut him off.

"I need you to take her from here tomorrow."

His head jerks back. "What?"

"There is a ship waiting to extract us in the ice world quadrant of the arena. If you can make it there, they will help you both escape."

"What about you?"

I shake my head. "I cannot make the journey. I will be in full withdrawal soon. You must leave me here."

"You will be killed," he says, as if I have not already considered this.

"I know." I swallow against the knot in my throat as I study her sleeping form. "But at least she will live." I turn to him. "I ask only that you take her to my people—to V'lora. We have an alliance with her world. They will help her return to her home planet."

His glowing orange eyes pierce mine as he studies me with a look I cannot quite discern. "I thought your people could not love. And yet... you truly love her, don't you?"

"Yes. I do." A dull ache settles deep in my chest as I

prepare to ask another favor of him. "I would ask something else of you, Lycaon."

"What is it?"

"I am T'Hale of the Great House of A'msir. I ask that you seek an audience with my father and my sister. Tell them what she is—" I stop short as I correct myself. "What she *was* to me. I do not know if her family even still lives. And I... know mine would take care of her if she needed anything... if she were to find herself completely alone."

"What makes you think she will go with me? That she will leave you behind?"

"I will convince her that I do not love her."

"She may not forgive you."

"It matters not," I tell him. "What matters is that you keep her alive. Do you understand?"

He gives me a solemn nod.

CHAPTER 38

VANEK

I lie back down beside Elena as Ryker lies down at the entrance of the cave. Morning light begins to creep in through the cavern, highlighting the varied and lovely shades of her chestnut hair.

I run my fingers through the long, silken strands, but quickly retract my hand as the tremors take hold of me once more. I grit my teeth against the agonizing pain that spears through me and my vision blurs as I study her, trying to memorize the contours of her face.

She is more beautiful than anything I have ever seen. I wish this moment would last forever. That I could hold her against me as I do right now.

Closing my eyes, I imagine a future of waking up to her each morning and falling asleep each night with her in my arms.

I lift my head and find Ryker studying me with a mournful gaze. I press one last kiss on Elena's forehead and then carefully untangle myself from her arms.

I kneel beside her and touch her shoulder to wake her. She opens her eyes and gives me a sleepy smile that I return with a stoic mask.

A small frown furrows her brow as she senses something is wrong. She sits up and looks at me with a questioning gaze. "What's wrong?" Her eyes widen when she notices Ryker behind me. A smile lights her face. "Thank goodness you're alive. When did you get here?"

He gives her a pained smile. "This morning. I have come to take you the rest of the way."

"You're going to travel with us?" She turns to me, her eyes full of hope. Her expression quickly falls as I stare back at her with an impassive mask.

"Ryker will look after you."

"What are you talking about? Where are you going? Are you going to try to lead the Hunters away?"

"Yes."

She takes my hand. "No. You have to stay with me. I don't want you to go. You could get hurt. You could die, Vanek."

I feel tremors about to begin, so I quickly retract my hand. She gives me a confused look. "What are you—"

"He is leaving because he knows his chances of survival are better without you," Ryker says, playing his part very convincingly. "Is that not true, V'loryn?"

I clench my jaw.

Elena shakes her head. "No, Vanek wouldn't do that. He loves me. He would never abandon me." She looks at me again. "He doesn't know you, Vanek. He doesn't know you like I do."

Ryker crosses his arms over his chest and levels an icy glare at me. "Are you going to tell her the truth?"

Actual rage boils in my veins at how convincingly he lies. I know I asked this of him, but it burns anyway.

"What truth?" Elena looks at me. "What is he talking about?"

Drawing in a deep breath, I prepare my lie. "I made a mistake."

"What kind of mistake? What are you talking about?"

"Us," I reply firmly.

She recoils as if slapped. "What do you mean 'us?' "

"I cannot take you as my mate. Nor do I want to."

She stares at me in disbelief. "Why are you saying this?"

"Because it's true. I do not love you. It was an act. I did it for the vidcams. I needed an ally in the arena, and I had you. You saved me in the river and now… I believe my chances are better alone."

"I don't believe you," she counters, her eyes full of hurt and betrayal. "You have taken care of me even before the Great Hunt."

"Because I knew the slavers would think we were a mated pair and they would put us together here in the arena."

She crosses her arms over her chest. "I don't believe you. You're lying, but why?"

"I am not lying."

Ryker walks over to her. "Come. We must leave here now before Hunters arrive. I can scent them on the wind."

"If you truly don't care about me, then why is he here?" She gestures to Ryker.

She is smart, but I had already anticipated this question. "To absolve me of any guilt related to your well-being. I am not a complete monster," I add coldly.

"I beg to differ," Ryker says darkly.

He moves to her side. "Come. We must leave. Now."

"No," she states firmly, blinking back tears. "I don't believe you. You're lying. You both are. But why? Why are you doing this?"

"It is not a lie," I grit my teeth, struggling against the wave of nausea and dizziness that washes over me. "It is the truth."

"No, it's not. Don't do this," she begs. "Please, Vanek. Don't do this."

I am at the edge of my control as the tremors break through. "Take her," I growl at Ryker. Now."

He grabs her forearm. "We have to go. Now."

"No!" she jerks away from him. "I'm not leaving you."

Unable to hold it together any longer, I double over in pain. I release a roar of frustration as I collapse on the floor and the world goes black.

CHAPTER 39

ELENA

I watch in horror as Vanek falls to the floor in a crumpled heap. "Vanek!" I drop to my knees beside him. Cupping his cheek, I turn his face to me. "Vanek, wake up!" I cry out, but he does not respond.

I whip my head toward Ryker. "What's wrong with him?" When he hesitates, I growl. "Tell me. Now!"

"He is going through withdrawals."

"From what?"

"Neural relaxers."

"How do you know this?"

"I saw the slavers give him pills on the ship. I confronted him about it while you were unconscious."

"Why didn't he tell me?"

"He did not want you to worry."

"We have to help him, Ryker. We can't just leave him here."

Ryker runs a hand roughly through his hair. "We could be caught if we stay in one place for too long."

"Can you help me move him?"

He shakes his head. "He is too heavy for me to get him safely down the cliff wall."

"He told you about the ship."

"We must reach it as quickly as possible."

"What if you go ahead? What if you find it first, and then… somehow come back for us?"

"I may not be able to."

"Well, try," I state firmly. "Because I'm not leaving him."

"You will be killed," he grinds out. "You cannot stay here."

I stand, tipping my chin up as I face him. "Vanek has watched over me all this time. Now, I will do the same for him."

Ryker huffs out a frustrated breath. "What would you have me do? I cannot just leave you here."

"You can and you will. But you will also travel to the mountain, find the ship, and come back for us."

Cocking his head to the side, he narrows his eyes. "Are all Terran females this stubborn?"

Despite my fears, a smile tugs at my mouth. "For the most part, yes."

I step closer to him, meeting his gaze evenly. "Please, Ryker. This is the only way we all make it out of here alive. I can't leave him. And I'm sorry to ask this of you, but I don't have a choice."

He looks at Vanek. "He might die anyway, and leave you here alone."

"It's a risk I'm willing to take," I state firmly.

Ryker gives me a subtle nod. "Fine. I'll go. I promise that I will return for you, no matter what it takes."

He truly is a good person. "Thank you."

He turns and leaves.

I lie down next to Vanek and wrap my arms around his trembling form as he curls in on himself. I wrap the blanket around him, trying to make sure he is warm as I run my fingers through his hair. "It's all right, Vanek. I'm going to take care of you, my love."

A deep frown creases his brow as he rasps. "You should have left me here, Elena. I—"

"I couldn't leave you. I'm going to stay with you. Ryker is going to the mountain to find the ship. You just have to hold on until he gets back, all right?"

He takes my hand and pulls it to his chest, directly over his beating heart. "Eh'leh-na," he whispers before he closes his eyes again and falls unconscious.

CHAPTER 40

ELENA

It's been two days since Ryker left. I'd thought Vanek's withdrawals would be similar to what I'd heard Terrans go through, but I was wrong. His consist of tremors, dizziness, shaking, chills, and bouts of unconsciousness, instead of vomiting and all the other horrible things Terrans go through when they suffer withdrawals.

I move to the far back part of the cave and take care of the pressing needs of my bladder. I'm glad for this alcove back here or else I'm not sure what I'd do.

When I return to Vanek, I lie down beside him as darkness falls outside. I pray there aren't any Hunters or predators nearby.

I tug the blanket up around us as I snuggle next to his shivering form, holding him close. "Is this better?"

Unable to speak, he nods.

I close my eyes as I lay next to him. I'm so exhausted. I've barely slept at all since Ryker left. We have plenty of supplies in our packs, but it's hard to rest knowing that we're being hunted and we can't leave this place. Not until Vanek is better or Ryker comes to retrieve us.

As hard as I try to remain awake, I finally fall away into the beckoning void of sleep.

Myriad images flow like a river around me. Some of them I recognize from my memories, but others I do not. I turn and find Vanek standing before me, but this must be a dream, because he appears completely fine.

"Not a dream," his voice whispers in my head. *"We are in the al'nara."*

A mournful cry echoes around us, and I spin to see Vanek in a dark uniform. His back is to me, and he's kneeling beside someone, but I cannot see who it is.

I start to walk toward him, but a hand grips my shoulder, halting me. *"Do not go there."*

I turn back to see Vanek behind me. I dart a glance back at his kneeling form to find his shoulders shaking with sobs as he leans over someone.

As I study that version of him, I see a flash of iridescent color and realize it is the reflection off a membranous wing. Vanek gathers a woman in his arms. Only a flash of her wing, and long, silver-white hair are visible. Her hand drops and I note the pale violet color of her skin. It's the Aerilon woman that haunts his dreams.

"That is Al'ora," he murmurs, his voice full of sadness.

"What happened to her?"

"I could not save her," he whispers. *"So, I offered her comfort in the only way I knew how."*

"What did you do?"

He stares at the image of him on the floor with Al'ora, his eyes fixed in a faraway look. *"I linked with her mind, in the al'nara. I wanted only to offer her peace as she crossed from this world to the next."*

His eyes fill with unshed tears. *"And in those last moments, I experienced her life, her pain and then finally her death."*

I inhale sharply.

The vision disappears to be replaced by the gardens on his estate—the ones he showed me before.

"This is where I go when the pain is too much. When it threatens to tear my soul in two."

My heart clenches, and I take his hand. *"Let me share your burden. You don't have to deal with this on your own."*

"For so long... it is as if I have been living in the darkness. And then I found you, Elena. Your kindness is like a candle in the never-ending dark. A light in a place that has long ago forgotten the sun.

"You are where the light begins in the darkness. You are everything to me. How could I bond with you, knowing I am so broken? It was a selfish dream. And you deserve better."

I cup his cheek. *"What I deserve is my decision, not yours. You believe you are not good enough, but I know that you are. Everything you have done, since the moment we met, has shown me that you are the man that I love. The man that I want."*

"Elena, I—"

A rumbling growl fills the air and my eyes snap open as I'm pulled back into sudden awareness.

Reflective yellow eyes with vertically-slit pupils meet mine in the darkness and my heart slams in my throat as I recognize the rifle in his hand and realize he is a Craven Hunter.

Lightning fast, Vanek moves to his feet and rushes toward him, slamming him against the wall and knocking the blaster from his grip. I reach for it, but the Hunter kicks it away and over the ledge. It goes tumbling down the cliff wall.

The Hunter twists in Vanek's grip, breaking free of his hold. He pulls a knife from his belt and jabs it at Vanek but misses as Vanek turns to one side.

It's easy to see Vanek is at a disadvantage as tremors move through his body as he clashes repeatedly with the Craven in a flurry of fangs and claws.

I pull the blade from my belt, and I know what I must do. I have to save Vanek. I grip the knife firmly in hand, waiting for an opening. I cannot fail. If I do, we're both dead.

Vanek pushes the Hunter away, slamming him against the cave wall just inside the entrance.

I race toward him, blade firmly in hand. He rushes back to Vanek, but I reach him first. Sinking the blade deep into the flesh of his back, I wrap my other arm around his neck, trying to knock him off balance.

He arches back, releasing a horrific roar of pain as he rushes back toward the wall. Pain explodes across my back as he slams me against the wall, but I refuse to let go.

Vanek stumbles toward us, barely able to stand. I can't let the Craven hurt him.

I kick back at the wall, pushing the Craven away from it. He loses his balance and I take advantage of his disoriented state and push my feet against the entrance, causing him to stumble back toward the ledge.

"Elena, no!" Vanek cries out as we fall over the side.

CHAPTER 41

VANEK

I watch in horror as the Craven stumbles toward the ledge, Elena still on his back. Her eyes lock on to mine and the world shifts in slow motion as they tumble over the edge of the cliff wall and toward the ground below.

"Elena!" I cry out.

Using all of my strength, I extend my claws and make my way down the mountain as fast as I can. I lose my grip and tumble the last several meters, slamming to the ground.

I turn and then gasp as I see Elena on the ground beside the Craven. He moves his head from side to side in pain, but I notice her chest rising and falling rapidly as she struggles to breathe.

I somehow manage to stand and stumble toward her, falling to my knees beside her broken form. "Elena," I whisper as I reach down and touch her face.

Tears stream down her face as she looks at me. She reaches a trembling hand out to me and I take it. "Vanek," she barely manages. "I think I'm dying."

I shake my head as tears blur my vision. “No, Elena. Please. You cannot die, my Si’an T’kara. Please, do not leave me.”

Her breath becomes shallow and her eyes are full of tears. I lean down and gently press my forehead to hers. “Please, my Elena. Please, do not die.”

Flits of memory surface in my mind. The memory of Marek using the Balance to restore Elizabeth’s life floods my thoughts. Elizabeth is his Si’an T’kara, just as Elena is mine. If he could save his bondmate using the Balance, so can I.

I take Elena’s smaller hand in mine. “I will save you, my Si’an T’kara.”

I place my other hand on the ground and dig my fingers into the earth. The raw and untamed energy like a beating pulse beneath my palm as I seek the life force of the earth around me.

The ground quakes with terrible force as I expand a circle all around us, drawing the life force of every living thing to me. Raw and primal energy burns like fire through my veins as I channel the energy to my beloved.

Through our connection, I can feel the energy spreading through her body, mending all her injuries.

I grit my teeth as I struggle to hold on, funneling the raw and burning life force to my Si’an T’kara. I refuse to give up. I will die or I will save her, but I refuse to let her go.

The goddess of death will either take us both or she’ll have nothing.

A pained roar escapes me as the last of the energy funnels to Elena, healing her broken form.

I glance down at her, and through our connection, I can sense that she is whole again.

Relief fills me so great, I can hardly contain it. Exhaustion steals through me, threatening to pull me under.

Her eyelids flutter open and closed as she struggles to stay awake. "Vanek," she whispers, gently squeezing my hand.

A blast of wind surrounds us, kicking up dust and debris. I lift my gaze to find a glider hovering above us. We are either saved or we are doomed.

I place myself protectively over my mate to shield her as it touches down. Barely able to remain conscious, I watch as the blurred figure of Ryken steps out onto the ramp and walks toward us.

Unable to stay awake any longer, my head falls back, and I tumble away into oblivion.

CHAPTER 42

VANEK

When I wake, it's to the familiar face of my friend Marek staring down at me as I lie in a medical bed. He runs a hand through his short, black hair and shakes his head as he looks at me. "Thank the goddess you are awake."

"Where am I?" Panic tightens my chest as I glance around and do not see Elena. "Where's Elena?"

My sister L'Tana steps out from behind him. Her long brown hair slips over her shoulders as she leans over the medical display, studying my readings. "She is resting in her quarters," she replies, matter-of-factly.

"How long have I been unconscious?" I sit up. "Is she all right?"

"You've been down for five days," Marek answers.

L'Tana arches a brow. "Of course, she is all right. I am an excellent Healer. She—"

"Don't forget me," Doc's voice calls out beside her.

She shoots him an irritated glance, and he grins, rubbing

the back of his head nervously. I notice a bead of sweat escape his short, black hair, but he brushes it away. It's so obvious to me and everyone else that this Terran is in love with my sister, as his cheeks flush red as she looks at him. "I helped too," he adds.

L'Tana arches a brow. "I did not mean to imply that you did not, Daniel," she tells him.

He grins. "I was just joking, L'Tana."

An answering smile quirks her lips.

Marek's bondmate, Elizabeth, steps forward, smiling brightly as her blue eyes meet mine. "We're so glad you're all right, Vanek. We were so worried."

I notice her long red hair is tied back from her face, and I wonder if she is still suffering from the Terran "morning sickness" with her pregnancy. "How did you find us?"

Marek glances over his shoulder at Taven. I had not noticed him before. With platinum hair and skin so pale you can see several green veins beneath, I don't know how I didn't see him before now.

He dips his chin in a subtle bow. "We found the last location of your distress call and I was able to track you to a certain point from there."

Taven is *ne'shal*. It is rare among my kind for anyone to have this ability. He is able to use his mind to reach out to others. Without him, we'd probably have died in the arena.

He continues. "Two Patikos contacted us as well, giving us the exact location of the planet you were on. When we arrived, we found both them and Ryker."

"What about the rest of my crew?" I ask. "Have you received any word?"

Marek looks at me. "All accounted for. The slavers only risked taking you and Elena. They believed she was V'loryn." He arches a brow. "That is how they listed her in the Great Hunt, as well."

"Were you able to free the other contestants?" I ask, hopeful.

Ryker is the one who answers. "All the slavers are dead and the slaves have been set free as well."

"Good," I reply, satisfied that the masters were executed.

I turn to Elizabeth and Doc—the two Terrans here. "Have you been able to locate Elena's family?"

"Not yet," Elizabeth answers. "She was among those who disappeared twenty-five years ago. She must have been kept in stasis sleep all that time, until recently."

Sadness tightens my chest. Terra went through a great pandemic only a few cycles before we made first contact with them. Her entire family could be gone. "Does she know how long it's been?"

"Yes," Elizabeth says sadly. "She does." She turns to Marek. "We've offered for her to stay with us until we find out something about her family."

"No," I quickly reply. "She will stay on the A'msir Estate with me." I shift my gaze to L'Tana, and she arches a curious brow but says nothing. "With *us*," I correct. "I'd like to see her. Can you take me to her?"

My sister steps forward. "There is something I must talk to you about, first." It doesn't escape my notice that she exchanges a worried glance with Marek. "It is important," she adds.

It is apparent that everyone but me knows what she means to speak to me about, because they all leave except for her and Marek.

"What is it?" I ask. "What's wrong? Is it something with Elena?"

L'Tana's eyes flash with anger. "How long had you been taking neural relaxers?"

I clench my jaw but do not answer. This is the conversation I hoped to never have with anyone.

"Tell me," she demands.

"Ever since I found Al'ora," I admit.

Marek inhales sharply. "But that was at least four cycles ago." Despite his impassive expression, sadness reflects in his gaze. "Why did you not come to me? I would have tried to help you, Vanek."

"There was nothing you could have done to help," I insist. "It was my fault. The Elders… they warn us against linking with other's minds. But I did not listen." Tears sting my eyes, but I blink them back. "I knew she would die the moment I found her… and I could not stand by and watch her suffer. It was the only way I knew to ease her passing. And even despite the nightmares I have endured since that day… I would do it again, if given the choice. She shouldn't have died." My voice breaks on the last word. "If we had gotten there sooner, she would still be alive."

Marek places a hand on my shoulder. "But we did not get there in time, and we never will. You cannot change the past." He pauses. "You offered a dying person comfort. And I do not believe she would have wanted such a kind and selfless act to end up destroying you, Vanek."

"You are right. I know that now, Marek." I draw in a deep breath. "I realized it when I nearly died in the Great Hunt." I look between him and my sister. "For the first time since that day, I realized just how much I want to live and how desperately I wanted to be free of my addiction. I want a life with Elena… a future."

"You can have one," L'Tana says softly. "The neural relaxers are cleared from your system. But you will have to find a healthy way to cope with all you have been through."

"I know." I swallow against the lump in my throat and look at them again. "Ryker told you what Elena is to me, did he not?"

They nod.

"She is my Si'an T'kara. I desire to take her as my bondmate more than anything I have ever wanted before, but I realize now that I cannot. It would be wrong to share my broken and damaged mind with her… subjecting her to the same nightmares that have scarred me so deeply."

"You know how I struggled with my fated bond to Elizabeth," Marek says. "You were the one who told me then that I would regret it if I pushed her away. So, now I am here, giving you the same advice you gave me." He pauses. "You were right, and I would have been devastated if I had ignored my heart."

L'Tana turns to me. "I have seen how much Elena cares for you… how much she loves you. Do not push her away unless you are entirely sure you can live with the consequences of that decision."

"How can I ask her to bond with me as I am?" I ask incredulously. "It was a foolish dream to think that I could take her as mine."

Taven steps out of the shadows, surprising all of us. I'd thought he was gone. "Forgive me." He dips his chin in a subtle bow. "As *ne'shal,* I could not help but sense the overwhelming despair of your thoughts. They are so forceful, I am having difficulty suppressing my abilities and keeping them out."

I sigh heavily. "Then it is I who should be asking your forgiveness, Taven. I do not mean to distress you."

His glowing green eyes meet mine evenly. "I would speak with you alone, if I could."

"Of course."

Marek and L'Tana exit the med bay, leaving us alone. "What is it you wish to say?"

"The ne'shal among our people were once hunted down and killed, hundreds of cycles ago," he begins, repeating a part of our peoples' terrible history that I wish had never happened. "My parents knew what I was and they taught me to hide my abilities… to suppress them as best I could. It can be… overwhelming to read the thoughts of everyone in the room and beyond."

His gaze sweeps to the opposite wall with a faraway look. "My parents put Tayla and I on one of the last ships before V'lorys was destroyed. There wasn't enough room for everyone, so they stayed behind. They lied to my sister and told her that they would get on the next ship."

Tears brighten his eyes. "I saw the truth in their minds. I also understood its purpose. They knew she would not get on the ship with me if she thought we would never see them again. And as our ship was leaving, I linked with my parents' minds, wanting only to spend every last second I could with them before—" His voice hitches.

"When the planet exploded… because I had opened my mind to reach my parents, I was unshielded from the hundreds of thousands of minds that had remained on the surface. In one devastating moment, thousands of voices cried out in terror in my mind."

My mouth drifts open in shock.

He continues. "I experienced the final terrifying moments of our people." A tear slips down his cheek. "And I have relived that day many times in my mind since then."

His eyes meet mine, full of intense sadness and pain. "I share this with you because I want you to understand something."

"What is it?"

"Traumatic experiences alter us irrevocably. There is no returning to the person you were before. It is impossible. People insist that you can overcome trauma, but it is much more complicated than that. It is not something you get through and then come out on the other side completely better and back to normal. It is something you learn how to carry.

"It is like walking every day with a heavy weight on your back. With enough time, you become accustomed to it and, although the weight has never changed, carrying it takes less effort." He looks down at his hands. "There are still days, however, where it feels heavier somehow, and it reminds you that you used to carry nothing."

His eyes lift to mine. "And those are the times that you seek out your person. The one you trust to carry it with you on those days so that the darkness does not swallow you whole."

"What would you do?" I ask. "If you were me?"

He clenches his jaw. "I have found my Si'an T'kara. She is Terran as well. I now face the same decision as you. And I have decided that I will tell her the truth. I will not make the decision for us both and take away her choice." He pauses. "I only pray she will choose me as her bondmate. I cannot bear the thought of being without her."

I rest a hand on his shoulder. "Thank you, my friend, for your counsel."

He dips his chin. "Of course. Now, come. I know Elena is anxious to see you." His lips quirk up in the hint of a smile. "Your sister had to force her to leave so she could rest. She refused even though it was evident she was so exhausted that she was near collapse."

As I follow him down the long corridor, I am nervous about seeing Elena. When we linked in the al'nara while I was in withdrawal, she got only a glimpse of my pain, and I am worried that it was more than she realized. She told me she wanted to help me to heal and I would help her, but perhaps in seeing some of my trauma, she may have changed her mind about becoming my mate.

We reach her door, and I activate the chime.

"Enter!" she calls out.

The doors whoosh open and Taven steps in first. "Taven." She smiles. "Have you come to take me back to Vanek? Is he—"

She stops short when I move out from behind him.

My heart hammers in my chest as her warm brown eyes study me a moment before a stunning smile curves her lips. She rushes toward me. "Vanek!"

CHAPTER 43

ELENA

As I stand before the floor-to-ceiling viewscreen, I stare out at the stars. Despite his sister's reassurances that he's all right, I'm worried about Vanek. I wish he would wake up.

L'Tana made me come here to rest, but I can't. Not when I know he's still in the med bay and unconscious.

I turn my gaze to the enormous bed. A massive, white, rounded canopy curves overhead, reminding me of a large, open cocoon. The bedding is covered with a shimmering silver material, embroidered in white thread with a thick pattern of curling vines full of heart-shaped leaves.

It looks so inviting but there's no way I'll be able to fall asleep. Not yet, anyway.

I move to the desk in the far corner, beside a table with two chairs. They appear to be made from ornately carved wood, lending an almost fairytale-like appearance to the space. Everything about this ship is a strange mixture of technology and intricately sculpted elegance.

It's almost as if I've stepped into some futuristic version of an Elven Kingdom.

I glance back out at the viewscreen again. It's been so long since I left Terra. Far longer than I thought. I wonder if my family is still alive. I can't imagine how terrible it was for them when I disappeared. They probably thought I was dead.

The door chime sounds, and I call out. "Enter!"

Taven steps in, and I greet him warmly, hoping he's come with news of Vanek or that he'll agree to help me find my way back to the med bay to sit with him while he sleeps.

Happiness blooms in my chest when Vanek steps out from behind him. I rush toward him, jumping into his arms. He catches me around my waist and gathers me to his chest before crushing his lips to mine in a searing kiss, stealing the breath from my lungs.

I'm not sure when Taven leaves. I only know that when we finally pull away from each other, he is gone.

Vanek's glowing green eyes meet mine, and I repeat the words in his native tongue. "Eh'leh-na, Vanek. Eh'leh-na, my love."

He cups my chin, tipping my face up to his. "You still want me?" Worry and uncertainty reflect behind his eyes.

"Yes," I reply without hesitation, because it's true. "I love you, Vanek. I want to be with you."

"You would be mine?"

I stretch up on my toes and wrap my arms around his neck. I press my lips to his and smile against them. "Yes."

"But I lied to you, Elena. I didn't tell you about my addiction."

"You were hurting, Vanek. And you were trying to shield me too. But you don't have to do that, my love."

His glowing green eyes search mine. "Forgive me," he whispers.

"I already have. But you have to promise me something."

"What is it?"

"If you ever find yourself in that place again… where you feel you have nowhere else to go… you have to come to me, Vanek. Don't run to something else, trying to mask your pain. Let me be your refuge, and you will be mine. Do you understand? "

"Yes," he replies solemnly.

"We have been broken, my love. But, together, we can heal. I love you, Vanek. And I want to be with you."

"Eh'leh-na, my Elena."

He gathers me in his arms and takes me to the bed. He gently lays me down beneath the sheets and moves over me. He leans down and kisses me long and deep.

I curl my tongue around his, deepening our kiss. He groans as I dip my fingers beneath the hem of his tunic and trace my hands up his chest and abdomen, exploring the hard planes of muscles.

His eyes meet mine, obsidian black and full of hunger. "Your scent is intoxicating," he breathes. "I want to taste you."

I recognize his statement is a question, and somehow, I manage to nod.

He quickly removes my clothing, leaving me in only my undergarments.

He pulls down my bra, freeing my breasts and then closes his mouth over the left peak. He laves his tongue over the hardened tip, and I arch up into him, wanting more.

He moves to my other breast and then continues down my body. He slips his hands beneath the waistband of my underwear and slides them down my hips.

His gaze holds mine as he guides my legs over his shoulders. He dips his head between my thighs, and my eyes roll up in the back of my head as he drags his tongue through my already slick folds and reaches the small pearl of flesh at the apex.

He growls low in his throat. "You are mine, Elena."

"I'm yours," I agree as I dig my heels into his back, writhing beneath his attention.

Banding an arm around my hips to hold me in place, he continues to tease his tongue through my folds, driving me mad with desire.

My entire body goes taut, and I cry out his name as my orgasm rushes through me like fire in my veins, leaving behind nothing but ash and devastation in its wake.

He presses a tender kiss to my inner thigh and then moves back up my body. Pulling me against him, he rolls us onto our sides, holding me close to his chest.

His l'ok is still hard between us. I cup his cheek. "You didn't—"

Gently, he tucks a stray tendril of hair behind my ear. "I want the first time I release to be when I'm inside you."

"You don't want to make love right now?" I ask, wondering why we've stopped.

"Before Elizabeth and Marek, we were not sure natural conception was possible between our two species. I did not want to assume that you would wish to risk conceiving," he explains. "I thought you might wish to speak with the Healers first about preventing—"

"What about a barrier method?" I ask.

He shakes his head. "V'loryn males… we knot inside our partners. The barriers your people use would break."

"Oh," my cheeks flare with heat.

He leans in and skims the tip of his nose along the curve of my neck and shoulders. A low growl rumbles deep in his chest. "Your scent is intoxicating. I believe you are nearing your fertile peak."

I blink several times. "You can tell that from my scent?"

He nods. "And I worry that my mating cycle is approaching, triggered by your nearness."

I think back on his explanation of the three to five days of repeated matings that occur during that time.

"We should reach V'lora within a few hours," he says. "If my mating cycle comes, and you are not ready to mate with me fully, I will seclude myself from you until it's over." He pulls me to his chest and breathes in a deep sigh. "Until then, I wish to hold you while you sleep, if you will let me."

Now that he's mentioned it, exhaustion runs through me. I haven't slept in at least two days, because I was so worried. Now that I know he's all right, I can finally relax and get some sleep.

"I love sleeping in your arms." I shift slightly to rest my head on his shoulder and my arm across his chest. "Are you sure you're comfortable like this?"

His glowing green eyes stare deep into mine with a look of love and devotion. "I would hold you forever if I could," he whispers, and my heart melts.

CHAPTER 44

ELENA

I lean back in Vanek's arms as we approach V'lora. I miss the familiar blue and white that defines Terra. V'lora is dominated by various shades of red and orange. As we move closer, dark patches of black and green punctuate the surface, but they are so minimal they are easily lost in the warmer colors.

Dozens of softly blinking lights catch my eye, drawing my attention away from the planet and to a mammoth structure off in the distance. The silver metallic structure stands out like a glowing beacon against a vast multitude of stars in the black void of space. "Is that the V'loryn orbital station?"

"Yes, that is A'tena Station."

My jaw drops. A'tena is massive compared to the Terran orbital station. But I suppose it has to be. Vanek says that almost all trade is conducted there. It is rare for any off-worlders to be allowed down to the planet's surface.

This is an added protection to guard the safety of their people ever since the destruction of their original home world—V'lorys. Less than half their population survived, so the safety of their citizens is the highest priority for their people.

Vanek presses a tender kiss to my temple. "My father has sent a dozen of our guards to meet us when we dock. We will then board a transport for the surface from the station."

It's still strange to me that Vanek is a noble Lord—a T'Hale, as his people call it. I've already met his sister. But now I'm nervous about meeting Vanek's father.

As we move closer, I notice the dozens of ships of varying shapes, colors, and sizes docked along the outer ring. More than three quarters of them are larger than any Terran space-faring vessel I've ever seen. "Are those all V'loryn ships?"

"Most. But many different species come here to trade for our L'sair crystals."

From what he's explained, the L'sair crystals are what the V'loryns and several other races use to power their ships and their cities. The fact that they are only found in the V'loryn planetary system means they are the wealthiest and most powerful compared to the other races.

A dull sound reverberates along the outer hull as the docking clamps attach to the ship. Vanek's hand on the back of my elbow steadies me as the slow yet abrupt stop makes me rock back on my heels.

I look across at him, so regally dressed in the colors of his House—a deep crimson red with the gold T'sar, panther-like sigil across his chest.

My own outfit was tailored to reflect them as well. L'Tana lent me some of her clothing. It was large on me, but one of the staff made a few adjustments to make certain it fit.

I was surprised that not only Vanek, but also his sister, made certain I had V'loryn clothing that identified me as part of their House, despite the fact that we are not bonded yet.

My black pants hug my legs and blend seamlessly into my

boots. My red, dress-like tunic is soft as silk against my skin. It looks almost ethereal as it floats softly behind me as I walk. The t'sar sigil is intricately woven in golden thread across the chest. It's beautiful. Like something out of a fairy tale.

My heart pounds as the metal doors slowly open to reveal at least a dozen V'loryn men—more of Vanek's guards.

The first one on the right steps up to greet us. With golden skin and short brown hair, his glowing green eyes widen slightly when I meet his gaze before it's quickly replaced by a typical stoic V'loryn mask.

Vanek claps a hand on his shoulder. "Garen, it is good to see you are well."

Crossing his arm over his chest, he bows deeply. "T'Hale. We were glad to receive word that you lived."

Vanek turns to me. "This is my future K'Sai, Elena," he says, using the V'loryn word that is equivalent to Lady. "Elena, this is Garen. The First of my Guard."

Garen bows low to me.

I give him a warm smile in greeting. "It is an honor to meet you, Garen."

"It is an honor to meet you as well, K'Sai."

The loud sounds of booted steps draw my attention off to the left to find Marek and Elizabeth, followed by at least a dozen of his guards. Their uniforms are similar in appearance to those of Vanek's men except displaying the dark gray and black color of Marek's house—D'enekai. Emblazed across their chest in silver thread is their House sigil of the v'rach—an animal similar in appearance to a dragon.

Ryker walks up to us with a smile on his face. "This is where we must part, my friends," he says with a sly grin. He winks at Vanek. "I know you're going to miss me, but try not to grieve too hard."

Vanek narrows his eyes, but then claps him on the shoulder. "We owe you a life debt, Ryker."

Ryker shakes his head. "Just promise not to let your people impound my ship next time my pack and I come to V'loryn space, and we'll call it even."

Vanek's lips quirk up. "Done."

"You've located your pack?" I ask.

He nods. "They should be here to pick me up within the hour."

"Thank you, Ryker," I tell him.

He nods. "I hope to see you two again but under better circumstances, of course."

Vanek's eyes dance with barely restrained amusement. "Of course."

We watch as Ryker walks away and into the crowd.

Vanek loops his arm through mine, and we move closer to Marek and Elizabeth as she does the same with her husband.

Both sets of guards surround us in a closed square formation. Elizabeth leans toward me and grins. "I know this probably seems a bit excessive, but V'loryns are very protective of their mates. This station has races from all parts of the galaxy, and they do not consider it as safe as the planet's surface."

"So, it's always this way when you come to the station?"

She nods. "Slavers pay thousands of credits for Terran, V'loryn and Aerilon women. It's just a precaution."

A small shudder runs through me. Suddenly, I'm immensely grateful for all the guards.

They form a tight barrier between us and everyone else. Although their faces are perfect stoic masks, it is easy to read their tension as we make our way through the station.

As if sensing my concern, Vanek takes my hand and sends a wave of reassurance and calm through the connection.

I can barely see much of the station over the shoulders of the guards. V'loryns are generally taller than mine, but because I'm not exactly a tall person myself, being surrounded by so many of his people, now, I feel so small.

Only able to glance at the upper levels that line the promenade, I'm surprised at not only how large it is but how impeccably clean and elegantly designed.

Soft light illuminates the entire station so bright it is as if we are standing beneath the sun. There are no sharp angles here. Rope-like, deep crimson vines cascade over the edges of the upper levels, lending an organic yet modern feel to the entire space. A rich, fresh, and earthy scent fills the station, reminding me of a forest.

Every surface is polished to a brilliant platinum hue so bright that even when I look down at the floor panels, my image is reflected back to me with sparkling clarity.

Each time the guards part just enough to allow me a small glimpse beyond their protective formation, I'm shocked at the myriad species that have come to trade here.

As we walk farther, the space opens up to reveal several more levels in concentric loops. The large area in the middle looks like a park. Covered in deep red, green, and purple vegetation, a small bubbling stream winds along one of the many inviting, tree-lined paths. The smell of heavy spices wafts through the air, rich and enticing. It's probably coming from the restaurant directly across from us on the next level up, full to overflowing with diners.

Several of the patrons turn in our direction, their eyes practically boring into us with their curious stares. A man with large sweeping horns and glowing lavender eyes flares his nostrils as his gaze zeros in on me. His skin flashes from stone gray to green and back again as his wings expand from his sides briefly before he tucks them against his back again. Leaning over the railing as if to look more closely at me, he grips the metal handrail, revealing long, lethal, black claws where a Terran's nails would be. He reminds me of a gargoyle like you'd see perched atop one of Terra's ancient structures—both strong and menacing. Despite my determination to appear unfazed, a small tremor of fear moves through me.

Vanek follows my line of sight to the gargoyle-like alien. "He is a Garkol. They appear menacing but they are mostly scholars. We are in talks with them to form an alliance."

His words set me more at ease, and I realize that I shouldn't be so quick to judge others based on appearances.

When we finally reach the transport, the guards split back into their respective houses as two transports await us. I hug Elizabeth goodbye and she whispers in my ear. "Come visit us soon. Our estate is just on the opposite side of the city from yours."

Our estate. It's so strange to think that Vanek and his family live in a literal castle, from what Elizabeth has explained to me.

Marek places his hand to her lower abdomen and gives her a concerned look. "Are you well, or has your nausea returned from the transport ride?"

She smiles warmly at him. "I'm fine, my love."

Vanek says goodbye to Marek and Taven, promising to meet up with them again soon.

He is so tender and gentle with her, just as Vanek is with me. I wave goodbye to them again and then step onto the transport with Vanek and his sister, L'Tana, and Doc, her Terran coworker who I'm suspecting is probably more than a friend, judging by the starry-eyed looks he keeps giving her.

Vanek helps me fasten the strange harness on my seat, and then takes the chair beside mine.

We take off, and for a minute, I'm nauseous at the sudden movement, but it quickly subsides.

As soon as we enter the atmosphere, the ship is steady

enough that we are able to stand and move to the viewscreen.

Vanek slips his arms around me and pulls me back against the solid warmth of his chest. The red-orange sun is so bright, I squint my eyes as we hover just above the surface. Tall, white buildings of exquisite and detailed architecture stretch out before us, reminding me a bit of ancient Terran European structures and yet more sleek and elegant in their design. Veins of gray and black streak through the marble-like stone, shimmering beneath the V'loryn sun.

"This is K'ylira—our capital city," Vanek explains.

It's so breathtakingly beautiful it's like some sort of futuristic fairytale. Various sleek glass and metal transports zip back and forth both in the sky and on the ground.

Vanek reaches around me and points in the distance. "Just beyond the edge of the city is our home, my Elena. I can hardly wait to show it to you."

CHAPTER 45

ELENA

As our transport flies over the capital, I stare out the viewscreen to the bustling city below. The V'loryn architecture, ornately beautiful, stands proudly in defiance of the sparse desert that surrounds it.

Vibrant green fields define the outer edges of the city. The sharp lines of vegetation marking the advance of the V'loryn efforts at terraforming this naturally red, barren planet.

Vanek says it will be at least three generations before the terraforming is complete, and this place resembles their old world—V'lorys—that was lost.

I turn to him and find his glowing green eyes studying me intently, a look of pure love reflected behind them. "There is so much I wish to show you." His gaze sweeps to the viewscreen before us. "Starting with our home."

My eyes follow his, and I'm speechless as the castle grows larger in the distance. I stare in wonder at the expanse of the sea-green ocean that expands behind it. The red-orange sun dips low on the horizon, scattering brilliant rays of light across the shimmering waves. It's nothing short of breathtaking.

"I didn't know you lived near the ocean," I tell him.

"The capital city spreads out along the edge of the main continent. Marek and Elizabeth's Estate is on the opposite side of the city.

"Our two Great Houses have always been close, even on V'lorys-that-was. Whereas the other Great Houses have separate territories far from here." He gestures to his castle in the distance. "Everything on V'lora has been constructed to look as it did on V'lorys-that-was. Our architects and engineers designed it this way when we settled here after the evacuation."

"Everything?" I ask, staring down at the city below.

He nods. "Even our estate and the surrounding gardens are the same as the ones I grew up in as a child on V'lorys."

When we reach the castle, the transport halts its forward movement. The floor vibrates slightly beneath us as we hover over the ground a moment before a low thud signals that we've landed.

Vanek takes my hand, and a low buzz of excitement thrums across the tenuous connection of our skin. The cool, saline breeze teases through my hair as we walk down the ramp and into an open courtyard filled with beautiful trees similar to Spanish Oaks.

Thick dark-gray trunks and branches twist up toward the sky as if competing for the sun. They are covered in heart-shaped leaves of various shades of orange and red. The grass beneath us is varying shades of lush green.

Vanek and L'Tana lead me around the side to an even larger garden in the back, facing the sea. I recognize the area with the blooming oralias from Vanek's mind when we linked the first time in the al'nara.

It's surrounded by a high wall of polished, white stone, lined with black-and-gray-streaked veins. Deep crimson vines hang over the side, swaying back and forth in the breeze like living curtains. They are dotted with small violet blossoms that span their entire length. Their blooms carrying a soft floral scent mixed with the crisp, salted air that surrounds us.

Tall, thick bushes of varying shades of purple and green bloom with vibrant petals surround us. If I'd never seen the planet's surface from the ship or the transport, I'd never know that most of it was a desert.

"This is all so beautiful, Vanek," I whisper.

He turns to me, a smile tugging at his lips. "I am glad you find it so."

He leads me through a massive set of doors that shimmer a moment before they disappear to reveal an opening.

Garen steps forward. His glowing green eyes meet mine, and he dips his head in a subtle bow. "Your father is eager to see you. He has requested you go to him as soon as you arrive."

Vanek looks to L'Tana and they exchange a nod. Doc walks up to my side. "Are you as nervous as I am?"

I frown, and he continues. "I've only met their dad once, but I'm not so sure he liked me."

A smile forms on my lips, and I whisper low as I watch Vanek and L'Tana speaking with one of their staff. "Are you and L'Tana together?"

His cheeks turn bright red. "I wish," he whispers in a voice so low I almost miss it. "I'm hoping that's why she invited me to dinner this evening."

Doc seems friendly, and I'm glad to have another Terran here. "Well, I'll cross my fingers for you that it all goes well."

He grins. "I'm going to need all the luck I can get." He

draws in a deep breath. "I've been in love with her for a while. I just hope she feels the same way too."

We enter into a large room with white stone flooring that seems to echo each step as we move farther inside. Bright light floods the interior from the floor-to-ceiling windows that completely line the opposite wall that looks out on the gardens and the ocean beyond it. The view is only broken by two wide and elegant staircases that curve along the side, winding up to the second floor where I notice a large terrace on the other side of the glass.

This space is sparsely decorated, aside from a few large tapestries of nature scenes along the walls.

Intricately carved light wood trim and baseboards run throughout the estate. Images of vines and flowers are etched in such fine detail that it appears as if they are growing along the corridors, lending an enchanting elegance to the interior.

If not for these soft architectural touches, this place would feel intimidating simply because of its enormous size. Instead, despite the lack of furnishings it feels almost cozy and warm in a way that I never suspected a castle might be.

As Vanek introduces me to each member of the household, I'm met with several fascinated stares. He makes sure to introduce me as the future K'Sai, and I'm surprised when they bow to me as if I already were his wife.

After I've been introduced to everyone, he leads me up a curved staircase to another floor and down a long hallway as we make our way to a double set of doors.

When we reach them, he gestures for me to raise my hand and press the panel beside them. Cautiously, I do so, and they shimmer and fade away, revealing a large bedroom. As soon as we enter, they seal behind us and blend almost seamlessly into the solid wall. "These are our rooms," he says, motioning to this one and another set of doors at one end.

"Rooms?" I blink several times in shock. "As in… more than one?"

"Yes."

I've only begun to scan the space when a low, rumbling growl draws my attention to the bed. I gasp as glowing green eyes stare back at me, and I recognize N'Sara from Vanek's memories.

Gracefully, she jumps off the bed and stalks toward us, her head low as she studies me warily.

Vanek kneels and holds out his hand. "N'Sara, this is my mate—Elena."

N'Sara cocks her large, panther-like head and then moves closer to me. I hold out my hand and her nostrils flare as she scents me.

After a moment, she ducks her head under my hand, as if asking me to pet her like a normal house cat would.

I smile as she rubs against my side and begins purring loudly in her chest.

Vanek arches a brow, amusement in his eyes. "I believe she likes you."

"Of course, she does," I tease. "She is obviously a very good judge of character."

He holds out his hand, and I take it without hesitation. "I want you to meet my father."

Drawing in a deep breath, I steel my nerves as we leave the bedroom. N'Sara pads along beside us, and I scratch gently behind her ear, glad for her company as we make our way to see Vanek's dad.

CHAPTER 46

ELENA

We walk back down the corridor and down the stairs to a large dining room. My gaze travels over the tall, vaulted ceilings and a long, rectangular table. A large hearth in the center full of L'sair crystals lends a soft warm glow to the room.

At the end of the long table sits a man that I can only assume is Vanek's father. He stands as we walk toward him. With short, dark-brown hair and warm, tan skin, he looks so much like Vanek that I would know this was his father anywhere.

His glowing green eyes study me intently, and he inclines his head in a subtle bow.

Vanek wraps a possessive arm around my waist as he introduces me. "Father, this is Elena Castillo of Terra. Elena, this is my father, Kyvak."

"I am pleased you are here," he tells me. "My daughter has told me much about you."

I'm surprised by this. I didn't spend much time with L'Tana on the ship.

She walks in with Doc, and I notice Doc's entire face is bright red by the time they reach the table. He extends his hand to their dad, and then quickly retracts it. "Sorry," he apologizes. "I forget sometimes that V'loryns don't shake hands."

Vanek's father arches a brow, and Doc's face turns even redder as we all take a seat at the table.

Staff bring in various platters of food, and I'm surprised to note a few Terran items, like strawberries, are available.

As if sensing my question, Vanek turns to me. "We have begun to trade food and various goods with your world. It has expanded our options for meals."

I notice Vanek's father seems rather pensive, even for a V'loryn. His stoic mask unable to hide the sadness I note behind his eyes.

Vanek is talking with L'Tana, but I can't help but think something is wrong with his dad.

As if sensing my gaze upon him, he lifts his head to me. "I wish their mother were here to meet you," he says softly. He darts a glance at Doc. "I think she would have liked him as well, you know. My bondmate was a very good judge of character and an excellent mother to our children."

N'Sara gently head bumps his hand, and he starts to pet her. He glances down affectionately at the t'sar. "I know you miss her too," he murmurs. He looks up at me again. "N'Sara always seems to know when I am sad. We spend much time together, she and I."

I smile. "She reminds me of a cat I had as a child."

He gives me a troubled look. "Has the Embassy been able to locate your family yet?"

Sadness fills me. "Not yet. But I'm hoping they will find them soon."

"Do you and Vanek plan to settle here?" he asks.

I'm surprised at his question because I hadn't even really thought beyond finding my family yet.

He continues. "I can have the east wing expanded if you'd like more space. And if you eventually decide upon children, we can add a nursery as well."

I think about how Vanek wanted to wait to make love because of the risk of us getting pregnant. I'm not sure how to respond because I don't even know if Vanek wants children. We haven't talked about it.

Vanek looks at his father. "Thank you, Father. But we have not discussed it yet."

When we're finished eating, Doc bids us goodbye to return to his apartment at the Terran Embassy in the capital. Vanek leads me out into the gardens overlooking the sea. He guides me to a bench near the oralias as we stare out at the water.

He turns to me. "I overheard my father speaking to you about where we might settle, but I would know your thoughts on the matter."

"What do you mean?" I ask. I'd just assumed he probably expected us to remain here. Especially since he is a T'Hale.

"Do you want to live here?"

"I—" I lower my gaze as tears fill my eyes. "I'm not sure I have anywhere else to go."

CHAPTER 47

VANEK

Her response troubles me, so I move to reassure her. "I do not want you to feel trapped here, Elena."

"It's not that," she says. "It's just… I feel out of place, you know." She gestures to the gardens and the castle. "All of this is new to me. And I just… feel like if I were to find my family, I could make a decision then. That I would have some sort of direction to figure out what I want to do."

Her answer suggests she has not entirely decided upon me just yet. I do not want to press her, so I simply listen as she tells me about her fears that her family is gone.

I only pray this is not so.

A staff member approaches. "K'Sai, there is a vid call for you from the Terran Ambassador."

She jumps up from her seat, and I do too. Quickly, we rush back inside and return to our rooms to take the call.

I tap a control on the screen and the Ambassador's face comes into view. He is a middle-aged man with peppered gray hair. He adjusts his glasses and then smiles brightly at her. "Elena Castillo. It is good to see you alive and well. We've located your family."

"You have?"

"Yes. Your sister and her daughter are on Mars Station."

Hope shines in her eyes. "What about my dad?"

His expression falls. "I'm afraid he is no longer alive."

She draws in a shaking breath as tears fill her eyes.

He quickly taps something on his display. "Your sister is waiting to be patched through. Shall I connect her to you now?"

Elena nods, and I hold my breath as the screen grows dark a moment before a woman with peppered gray hair appears on the screen. She appears just like Elena, but older. Twenty-five years older, I realize.

A younger woman sits beside her. She looks so much like Elena, they could be sisters as well, but I suspect it must be her niece.

"Elena?" She chokes back a sob as tears stream down her cheeks. "Elena, is it really you?"

"Emilia." Elena's voice quavers. "I've missed you so much."

A man with silver hair appears behind her, and he smiles at the screen. "Emmet?" Elena says, her voice full of disbelief. "Is that you?"

He laughs softly. "Older and more handsome than when you last saw me, but yes," he teases. He wraps an arm around Emilia and their daughter. "This is Elena, our daughter."

Emilia can barely speak through her tears. "We named her after you."

I observe as they cry tears of joy at their reunion. Elena places her hand on the screen and her sister does the same. Her shoulders shake with sobs. "I was so afraid you were already gone," Elena's voice quavers. "When I found out how long it had been, I thought—" her breath hitches. "How did dad die?" she asks. "What happened?"

Her sister can barely speak through her tears. "It was peaceful," she reassures her. "He never gave up hope that you were still alive. He knew you'd come home someday."

My heart clenches as they continue to cry. Her sister tells her stories about her life and their father.

Elena turns back to me and takes my hand. "Emilia, this is Vanek. He saved me," she says.

I notice she does not introduce me as her bondmate, and it worries me, but I say nothing.

"Thank you, Vanek," Emilia says. "Thank you so much for bringing her back to us."

Emmet steps closer to the screen. "We have an extra room in the house and plenty of space for you to move in with us, Elena."

My heart stutters and stops. Instead of telling them she wants to stay with me, she thanks them.

A deep ache settles in my chest. I love Elena, but I would never ask her to stay with me if she has changed her mind.

My wrist comm beeps, and I excuse myself to answer my sister's call, leaving Elena to speak with her family.

I walk out into the hallway to find L'Tana. "Is she going to stay?" she asks. "Or will she leave to be with them?"

"I… do not know," I answer honestly. "They were just discussing it."

"Vanek, have you asked her to bond with you yet?"

"I've told her that I want to, but… we haven't spoken of it since we got here. And now… I don't know if this is what she wants."

"You must ask her."

I clench my jaw as she says this as if it were something easy to discuss, when in truth, I'm afraid to even broach the subject. Especially after our talk in the gardens. I'm worried she'll tell me she has changed her mind about us, and that she wants to leave.

By the time I walk back in the room, she is already asleep on the bed, having finished speaking with her family. I sigh heavily, knowing she is exhausted but still desperate to speak to her.

I carefully pull the blanket over her shoulders and then curl myself around her sleeping form. Instinctively, she turns and nestles against me. My heart clenches. I am so afraid she will not want me anymore. Why would she? I am broken.

Closing my eyes, I allow myself to fall away into sleep.

CHAPTER 48

VANEK

An intoxicating scent floods my nostrils and my eyes snap open. My gaze travels over Elena's sleeping form, and I lean my head in, scenting along her neck and shoulders. My fangs extend as desire courses through my veins like fire.

Sudden dread douses the flames when I realize what this is. Elena's scent indicates she is fertile, and it has triggered my mating cycle.

I quickly remove myself from the bed and out into the hallway to find my sister. She will have to sedate me, and I will seclude myself as far from Elena as possible. I cannot bind her to me. Not when she has not yet decided if she wants to be mine.

CHAPTER 49

ELENA

When I wake, I notice Vanek is not beside me. I go out into the hallway and find his sister sitting in a chair outside.

"Where's Vanek?"

"He wanted me to wait for you. He has entered his mating cycle and secluded himself in another part of the estate."

"Why?"

She arches a brow. "He did not want to press his… needs upon you since he was unsure you still wanted him."

"Of course, I want him. I love him."

She purses her lips. "He does not know that."

"Take me to him. Please."

"It is best to let his cycle run its course. I will try my best to keep him sedated, but if he starts to have problems… I will have to contact the Elders."

"Why?"

"V'loryn males sometimes have to bond to a partner during their cycle or else they run the risk of going mad."

"What?" I ask incredulously.

"It is rare, but it can happen." She pauses. "When it does, the Elders find a mate for them to bond with as soon as possible."

"I don't want him to bond with anyone else," I state firmly. "I love him."

She appears unconvinced. "I overheard your conversation in the garden. You did not sound sure of staying with my brother."

"I just... didn't know what I wanted to do with my life outside of my relationship with him. I would like to have a job. To work and do something during the day. It's just who I am."

"Then you were not questioning whether or not to stay with him?" she asks, a hint of skepticism in her voice.

"No," I deny vehemently. "Now, take me to him. I want to see him."

"You will not want him like this," she says. "He may not be gentle and—"

"Take me to him now," I state firmly. "Or else I'll find him myself."

She dips her chin and leads me down the hallway to another set of rooms.

She opens the door, and I step inside, sealing the door shut behind me.

CHAPTER 50

ELENA

As soon as it shuts, I see Vanek standing across the room.

His glowing green eyes are swirling with black as they study me. "You should not be here," he says in a low voice. "You need to leave."

"Why?"

"It is not safe."

I walk toward him, but he steps back. "What's wrong?"

A deep growl rumbles in his chest. "You need to leave." His voice is rough as he speaks. "Now, Elena."

"Why? Because of your mating cycle?"

He nods. "I desire to claim you more than anything, but I will not bind you to me if you do not want me, Elena. Please, leave now before I lose my control."

"I love you, Vanek, and I want you. I trust you. You won't hurt me. I know you won't."

"You do not understand," he grinds out. "During our mating cycle, it is difficult to maintain control. It is three to five days of repeated matings. If I take you now and seal you to me, I do not know how much control I will have. I could hurt you." He pauses. "You have been through so much, I do not want to take you roughly."

"I trust you, Vanek." I walk over to him, standing in front of him as I search his eyes. "You won't hurt me."

"Please, Elena." His hand trembles as he touches my cheek. "You must leave now, while you still can."

"No." I stretch up on my toes and wrap my arms around his neck, crushing my lips to his.

At first, he doesn't move, but after a moment, he slips his arms around me and pulls me close, returning my kiss with equal fervor.

"Vanek," I breathe between kisses. "I love you. I want to be with you."

"Elena," he breathes my name out like a sigh.

I curl my tongue around his, and he lifts me into his arms, pressing my back against the wall as his mouth meshes repeatedly with mine.

"I want you, Vanek. I love you and I want to be yours."

He kisses me long and deep, stealing the breath from my lungs.

When he pulls back, I'm breathless and panting. I touch his face, tracing the sharp line of his brow as I stare deep into the eyes of the man I love.

He strokes my cheek, pain etched in his normally stoic features. "Goddess, help me, I cannot push you away."

"Then don't."

"You do not know what you are saying," he rasps.

"I want you, Vanek. Bind me to you, my love."

Something inside him snaps. His mouth covers mine in a searing kiss as he carries me to the bed. Gently, he lays me down on the comforter then crawls over me. He extends his claws and slices a line down the fabric of my clothing, leaving me completely bare beneath him.

His gaze holds mine as he runs his hands lightly down my already sensitive skin, staring at me in reverence. "You are perfect, Elena."

I reach up, tracing the chiseled planes of his abdomen and chest—pure, masculine perfection.

My eyes drop to his length, hard and erect, a bead of liquid gathering on the end. I carefully brush my thumb over the tip. His eyes swirl from glowing green to obsidian as I mark my abdomen with his essence.

His nostrils flare as his fangs extend, and I realize it is taking every bit of his control to remain still. "You are mine," he growls.

He kisses me passionately before pressing a series of suctioning kisses down the length of my body. When he drags his tongue through my folds, I arch up against him as he concentrates on the small bundle of nerves at the apex.

He growls low in his throat, and the vibration ripples straight through me, sending shivers of pleasure directly to my core. He takes my hand, threading his fingers through mine. The connection flares brightly between us, and I moan as desire pulses strongly across the link.

Something dark and primal uncoils from deep within him, clawing beneath the surface of his mind, desperate to break through and claim me as his mate. I can feel his struggle to hold it back, afraid that he will scare me.

"I want all of you, Vanek. I'm not afraid," I whisper. "I trust you. Completely."

He continues to tease his tongue around the softly hooded flesh between my thighs, and I reach for him, running my fingers over the tips of his pointed ears. My entire body goes taut like a bowstring, and then I'm coming harder than I ever have before.

I'm restless and panting as he glides up my body. I gasp as the crown of his length bumps against my entrance. The breath stutters from my lungs as he pushes into me. Everything is tight and uncomfortable at first as my body stretches to accommodate his length.

He freezes, his expression full of worry. "I do not want to hurt you."

"I'll be fine, my love. I just need a moment to adjust."

My body slowly relaxes around him, and he begins to advance once more.

I moan and dig my fingers into his back as he rocks his hips back and forth until he's fully seated inside me.

"So tight," he rasps.

Through the touch of our skin, I can sense he's on the razor-sharp edge of his control, struggling to hold back for fear he will hurt me.

"I trust you, Vanek. Bind me to you, my love."

He presses his mouth to my own, curling his tongue around mine and deepening our kiss.

I wrap my arms and legs tighter around him, holding him close. I love the feel of his body over mine, and the way he moves deep inside me.

Nothing exists outside of this moment and the connection of our souls. He rips his mouth from mine and sinks his fangs deep into my neck.

His mind flows into mine as we fall deep into the al'nara. *"You are mine, and I am yours."*

"I am yours, and you are mine."

We swim through the ocean of our combined thoughts, and as he begins to stroke inside me, my pleasure heightens at the experience of every sensation as he thrusts deep in my channel.

The ridges of his length create the most delicious friction, and my toes curl as each stroke into my body becomes longer, deeper, and more forceful.

He growls in arousal as he experiences my pleasure, the sensations moving between us in a feedback loop driving my desire even higher, and I'm lost in overwhelming bliss.

As I feel the gentle pull on my skin as he drinks my blood, I hold him close, threading my fingers through his hair.

"Mine," he breathes against my skin as he pulls away. He swipes his tongue over the two puncture wounds and seals them. "Eh'leh-na, my Elena."

He drops down low, wrapping his arms around my waist and holding me so close there is no space between our bodies.

"You are mine." He groans as he drives deep within me.

I trace my hands down his back, feeling the powerful muscles with each thrust as he claims me completely.

I gasp as everything becomes tighter somehow, almost to the point of pain but not quite. It expands into intense pleasure that steals the breath from my lungs. "What's happening?" I barely manage.

"My knot is expanding," he grits through his teeth.

I've never felt so full. A low moan escapes me. My lips part, and my entire body locks up before I fall over the edge. As ecstasy washes over and through me, I cry out his name.

"Mine!" he roars above me, his length pulsing strongly as he fills me with the delicious warmth of his seed. It feels as though it goes on forever. And just when I'm coming down from my orgasm, he pins my hands to the mattress beside me as he strengthens our connection.

I gasp then shudder as his length pulses again, and he erupts deep inside me, my body clenching around him, pulling his seed deep into my womb.

I'm breathless and quivering as he rolls us onto our sides, his length still knotted deep in my channel. He tenderly brushes the hair back from my face as I blink several times, fighting fatigue as my body lies spent beside his.

He seals his mouth over mine in a claiming kiss then begins to move deep inside me again. I pull back just enough to meet his gaze. “You want me again so soon?”

“Yes,” he rasps. “I need you.”

He rolls me beneath him, and my lips part in a low moan as he begins to stroke inside me once more.

CHAPTER 51

ELENA

When I wake the next morning, I'm wrapped up in Vanek's arms. I turn to face him, wincing slightly at the dull ache between my thighs, a reminder that my V'loryn bondmate has thoroughly claimed me.

He skims the tip of his nose alongside mine, then presses a tender kiss to my lips. I run my fingers through the hairs at the nape of his neck.

He pulls back to regard me and gently touches the mark he gave me. "Can you feel my presence in the back of your mind, my Elena?"

The gentle hum of his consciousness fills me with warmth. "Yes, my love. I can."

I reach up and touch his face, tracing the handsome line of his jaw. "I love you, Vanek."

He pulls me closer to him, and I wince slightly.

He glances down at me. "Did I hurt you?"

"I'm fine, my love. Just a bit sore."

Guilt shines in his eyes. "I should have been more careful with you. I—"

I press a finger to his lips to silence him. "It's all right, my love. I'm fine."

He nods and then rises from the bed.

I marvel at the perfection of his body. The thick, corded muscles flex as he scoops me into his arms and carries me to the cleansing room. We stand beneath the shower, and then he wraps a warm robe around us both.

"It is tradition to greet the dawn the morning after our first joining," he says. "It symbolizes the beginning of our lives together, as one."

"That sounds beautiful, Vanek." He carries me out onto the balcony and settles me in his lap.

I relax back against the solid warmth of his chest as we watch the first yellow-orange rays of the sun rise over the ocean in the distance.

He cups my chin and turns my head back to his, brushing his lips against mine in a loving kiss.

I turn in his arms to face him, straddling his hips.

Wrapping my hand around his l'ok, I position him at my entrance. He groans as I lower myself onto him until he's fully seated deep inside me. His gaze holds mine intently as he begins to move his hips against mine. "You are mine, Elena," he whispers. "And I am yours."

EPILOGUE

ELENA

As I lie in Vanek's arms, he hugs me tightly to his chest. I had a nightmare last night, but, together, we worked through it. Just as I help him to work through his.

"What are you thinking, my love?" I ask softly.

"That I never knew it was possible to experience such joy," he whispers.

I smile brightly at him. Cupping the back of his neck, I pull his lips to mine.

He kisses me long and deep, and then dips his head to the curve of my neck and shoulder, inhaling deeply of my scent. When he pulls back, his eyes swirl from glowing green to obsidian black. "I can scent your need, my Elena."

He captures my lips in a searing kiss then rolls me beneath him.

He kisses a heated trail along my jaw and from my neck to the valley of my breasts, moving with sensual slowness down my body to lave his tongue over one soft peak. It turns into a sensitive, hardened bead beneath his attention. I moan as he travels lower, already anticipating what will happen next.

He goes still, and I lift my head. "What's wrong?"

His nostrils flare as he scents my lower abdomen, and his eyes widen when they meet mine. "You are carrying our child," he whispers, his voice full of wonder.

My heart stops. It's only been a few weeks since his mating cycle. "Are you sure?"

"Yes. Your scent has changed."

As he places his open palm over my abdomen, happiness floods across our bond. "I can already sense the lifespark of our child in your womb."

Tears escape my lashes as I rest my hand over his.

"Why do you cry, my Elena?" He stares down at me with worry.

I cup his cheek. "I'm crying because I'm so happy, my love."

He captures my mouth in a claiming kiss, whispering in my mind. *"Eh'leh-na, my Elena. I love you so much, my Si'an T'kara."*

He kisses me long and deep, making love to me so tenderly it brings tears to my eyes.

And afterward, when I fall asleep, he meets me, as he often does, in my dreams, linking with me in the al'nara.

~

Strong arms encircle me as I lean back into the arms of my bondmate and husband, no longer hidden from me in shadow.

I turn back and smile up at him. "I knew you would find me here."

He holds me tight against him and whispers in my ear, his voice smooth and deep. "I will always find you, my Si'an T'kara."

"Stay with me," I whisper. "Don't leave me here alone. I sleep better when you're here."

"So, do I," he replies softly.

He holds me close and whispers words in the ancient tongue of his people. And although I do not understand them, I know what they mean by the way they leave his mouth in a breathless whisper.

"You are my Si'an T'kara. I will never leave you." He places his palm over my abdomen. "You are my light, my refuge, and my greatest love, my Elena. And I will always be yours."

ABOUT JESSICA GRAYSON

If you enjoyed this book, please leave a review on Amazon and/or Goodreads.

Want more V'loryns? Check out my V'loryn series with Marek and Elizabeth or my Ice World Warrior Series.

V'loryn Series (Vampire Alien Romance)

Lost in the Deep End

Beneath a Different Sky

Under a Silver Moon

Do you like Dragon Shifters? Elves? Fae? Vampires?

Ice World Warrior Series

Claimed: Dragon Shifter Romance

Bound: Vampire Alien Romance

Rescued: Fae Alien Romance

Stolen: Werewolf Romance

Taken: Vampire Alien Romance

Fated: Dragon Shifter Romance

Fairy Tale Retellings (Once Upon a Fairy Tale Romance Series)

Taken by the Dragon: A Beauty and the Beast Retelling

Captivated by the Fae: A Cinderella Retelling

Rescued By The Merman: A Little Mermaid Retelling

Bound To The Elf Prince: A Snow White Retelling

Claimed By The Bear King: A Snow Queen Retelling

Protected By The Wolf Prince: A Red Riding Hood Retelling

Want Dragon Shifters? You can dive into their world with this completed Duology.

Mosauran Series (Dragon Shifter Alien Romance)

The Edge of it All

Shape of the Wind

V'loryn Holiday Series (A Marek and Elizabeth Holiday novella takes place prior to their bonding)

The Thing We Choose

For information about upcoming releases Like me on Facebook at Jessica Grayson http://facebook.com/JessicaGraysonBooks.

Made in the USA
Columbia, SC
06 July 2025

60387511R00145